Winning the Blacksmith

LOVE IN APPLE BLOSSOM
BOOK SIX

KIT MORGAN

Winning the Blacksmith

(Love in Apple Blossom, Book 6)

© 2023 Kit Morgan

Cover design by Angel Creek Press and EDH Designs

✿ Created with Vellum

License Note

This book is licensed for your personal enjoyment only. This book may not be re-sold or given away to other people. If you would like to share this book with another person, please purchase an additional copy for each recipient. If you're reading this book and did not purchase it, or it was not purchased for your use only, then please return and purchase your own copy. Thank you for respecting the hard work of this author.

Chapter One

**pple Blossom, in the Montana Territory
1879**

Three weeks.

It was amazing what could happen in three weeks. The days, though still warm, had a crispness now in the mornings. Agnes Featherstone got grouchier, and the little town of Apple Blossom still didn't have a doctor. But that wasn't as concerning as that it also didn't have a preacher. Harold Watson and Captain Montgomery Finbar Stanley had been taking turns teaching a town Bible study on Sundays, but it wasn't the same as a real preacher, and though both men were well versed in the Bible, neither felt qualified to shepherd the tiny town.

Then there was the problem of five unwed couples

1

who were growing more impatient by the day. Captain Stanley made another trip to Virginia City to check if he had any takers to an advertisement he'd placed in the town's newspaper. So far there was nothing.

"I can't understand it," the captain told Oliver Darling as he scratched his balding head. "Who wouldn't want to come to Apple Blossom and preach?"

"Well," Oliver hedged, "it *is* quite small. Perhaps if Apple Blossom had more to offer?"

"What?" the captain snapped. "But we have everything one could need. There's a general store, and now with Mr. Hawthorne here, we'll have a hardware store too. Mr. McSweeney is cooking at the hotel so folks can dine there if they want, and he'll do the same in the saloon once he has the kitchen to his liking. There's a great fishing hole nearby, plenty of apples around to pick, and we have Woodrow Atkins' sawmill for folks that need to build a house." He downed his mug of milk. "We even got a saloon. I may not have customers, but I enjoy it."

Oliver did his best not to laugh. The captain was an odd sort, but kindhearted and generous. "The town needs a schoolhouse."

"That's easy to remedy. Want to help me build one?"

"Me? But I'll be leaving soon."

"Ha!" He poured milk from a pitcher into Oliver's mug. "What about the weddings? You'll want to stay for those."

"But Phileas will be going home to inform our parents what's happened."

Captain Stanley laughed. "You mean all the falling in love? I'd like to see the looks on their faces when he tells them."

Oliver cringed. He dreaded that moment. Father would ask a lot of questions. But Mother... the screams of protest would be heard across the county and into the next.

Captain Stanley slapped him on the back. "Cheer up, Ollie. You'll have a nice trip back to England, then get to return to Apple Blossom as soon as Phileas has said his piece."

Oliver rolled his eyes. "Mother is liable to chain me in the attic."

"Come now, she can't be that bad."

"You don't know our mother. She'll be sorely disappointed my brothers married women not of her choosing. Then she'll set her sights on me. I'll not have a choice." He crossed his arms over his chest. "With my luck she'll try to marry me off to Laurel Finchbottom."

Captain Stanley spewed milk. "Who?"

Oliver heaved a sigh. "Laurel Finchbottom. Her father's an earl."

"Won't you be marrying up?"

Oliver laughed. "Well, sort of, and the Finchbottoms are wealthy enough."

"Is she pretty?"

Oliver left the table and paced in front of the bar. "Yes, but it's those dratted brothers of hers. They never let her out of their sight and worse, they don't care for

3

my brothers and me. Ever since Sterling and Phileas filled their boots with rotten duck eggs, they've had it in for us."

Captain Stanley laughed. "Duck eggs?"

"Emphasis on *rotten*." Oliver stopped before the table and sipped his milk. "Laurel has six brothers. She's the youngest, and beautiful. But the rest ..." He shuddered.

"That bad, eh?"

"You have no idea." Oliver set his mug down and sat. "There are, of course, other young ladies in the county my mother has her sights on. But after being here, and watching my brothers get themselves paired off so... naturally, I don't know if I could stand having dozens of women paraded before me."

Captain Stanley smiled. "I wouldn't mind."

Oliver sighed. "Yes, but to have someone else pick for you..."

The captain slammed a meaty fist on the table. "Now see here, lad. Can't you pick your own wife?"

"Without my mother interfering? No. It can't be done."

"Why not? Don't tell me you're afraid to stand up to the woman?"

"Not at all. It just won't do any good." Oliver folded his arms on the table and rested his chin on them. "My mother is frightening beyond belief. Even the village magistrate is afraid of her."

Captain Stanley's eyes bulged. "You don't say?"

Oliver nodded and turned his mug this way and that. "I don't know how our father has survived all these years. Of course, Mother loves him dearly, but still. Anyone that can strike fear into the local magistrate must be a harbinger of death."

"Oh, for the love of Pete. She can't possibly be that bad. I've never heard your brothers speak of her like this."

"That's because my brothers are all marrying women of their choosing. By the time our mother finds out, there will be nothing she can do about it. They'll all be wed."

"Hmmm," the captain said as he scratched his beard. "That is a problem. Unless, of course, you find yourself someone to marry before you go?"

Oliver raised his head, then let it plop back onto his arms. "There's no one left in Apple Blossom to marry."

"Nonsense, there's Alma."

Oliver's eyes went wide as he straightened.

Captain Stanley made a face. "Oh, all right, she talks and talks. Well, what about Etta?"

"She smells of horse all the time."

"Of course she does, she's the blacksmith." He topped off Oliver's mug. "Have another cookie." He shoved the plate toward him.

Oliver took one. "I'm afraid I'm doomed, captain." He waved the cookie around. "Doomed to bear the brunt of my mother's fury." He took a generous bite and chewed.

Captain Stanley eyed him a moment. "Maybe you

should give Etta or Alma a chance."

He shook his head. "I'd rather take my chances with Laurel Finchbottom's brothers."

"Well, if that's the way you feel about it." The captain took a cookie and tore a piece off. "But mark my words, young man, don't make the mistake of passing up what's right under your nose."

Oliver ate the rest of his cookie in silence. Alma would talk him to death, and Etta, well, she not only smelled of horse, but half the time there was a fishy odor that lingered around the blacksmith's shop. He didn't know what it was from and didn't want to. Etta's face was always smudged with dirt and who knows what else, and he wondered how often she took a bath. Her clothes were torn, her boots worn, and did she own a comb? A few times he'd seen her looking decent and had to admit she was pretty. If only she'd keep herself that way instead of looking like a... well, a blacksmith.

"I'm sure we'll hear from our new preacher any day now," the captain said optimistically. "Then your brothers can marry, and you can make your little trip to England. Who knows, maybe this Laurel and her brothers will be nice to you."

Oliver tried not to sigh and reached for another cookie. He should get back to work. Now that the hotel was almost completed, he could get started on... "Oh, bother."

"What?" Captain Stanley shoved the rest of his cookie into his mouth.

"I've got to start work on Etta's place. She's next on the list."

The captain's eyes narrowed. "You don't sound thrilled."

He shrugged. "I'm sorry, it's just that I don't relish working on the livery stable and smithy. Phileas will be less than pleased if he has to help."

The captain rolled his eyes. "Working on Etta's place doesn't mean you have to fall in love. If she's not your type, then get the work done and move on."

Oliver stared at him a moment. Captain Stanley was right. Just because his brothers all fell in love with the owners of the places they were working on didn't mean he had to. He smiled at the thought and took another cookie.

Etta Whitehead cast her line, then propped her fishing pole on a rock and held it in place with another. She enjoyed fishing alone and the peace it offered. Other times she went to fetch Billy Watson to see if he wanted to go with her. The boy helped her keep her mind off her troubles. At seven, he was clever and witty and came up with all sorts of things to make you think.

But today she wanted to be by herself and hoped things stayed quiet. She'd had another nightmare last night and didn't want to think about it. Still, running from her fears would not make them go away. They'd just chase her harder, and when they caught up to her she'd have to be ready. Today hopefully wasn't that day.

She closed her eyes and let the warmth of the sun soak into her face. If she got too hot, she could always take a swim. Today was Wednesday, and no one ever showed up at the shop on a Wednesday. She always straightened things up in the livery stable, then came here.

Tomorrow would be busy. On Thursdays Mr. Smythe and his wife came to town and always stopped by the shop for this or that. Letty Henderson's horse Sir Charles needed shoeing, and she was supposed to bring him by tomorrow as well. Sterling Darling might bring him instead, and if he did, she could ask when he and his brothers were to begin work on the shop. The youngest inspected it what seemed like ages ago and she hoped they hadn't forgotten about her. She knew she had little, but what she did could use a few repairs.

Etta sat up, checked her pole, then shaded her eyes against the sun. She was already warm and could use that swim about now.

She slipped behind some bushes, stripped down to her chemise and bloomers, then headed for the water. She went downstream a piece and waded in, not caring if she scared the fish. Cooling off was more important than catching her dinner right now.

She reached the deepest part of the swimming hole and did her best to float on her back and tread water. This was her idea of Heaven: hot, late summer days, her favorite fishing spot, and a nice cool swim. Smithing was hard work and she sometimes wondered how long she'd be able to do it. She was small-boned, shorter than a lot of the women in town, and, next to Jean Campbell, probably owned the least number of things. But Jean still had a decent building to work out of. One made exceptionally grand by Wallis Darling and his brothers.

Now that Jean and Wallis were getting married, they were going to purchase Sarah Crawford's place. Sarah was marrying Irving Darling, who'd purchased the building next to the bank, a good-sized two-story structure with living quarters on the second floor and a storefront below. They wanted to turn it into a bakery. Jean and Sarah would run it and Jean would take care of the town library in her spare time.

Sterling, the eldest Darling, was marrying Letty Henderson and would live on her ranch outside of town. Conrad Darling was to marry Sheriff Cassie Laine and was already working as her deputy. And of course, Dora Jones, who ran the hotel, got a proposal from Phileas Darling after he began working full-time on her place. All five couples were happy in love and waiting not so patiently for a preacher to come to town to marry them. If they had to wait much longer, Etta had no doubt they would travel to Virginia City to see to their nuptials.

She dove under water. There would be no nuptials for her, but she didn't care. She would make it on her own just fine. So long as she kept quiet, did her work, and didn't bother anyone, she would remain in Apple

Blossom as the town blacksmith until she got too old and weak to do the job. Then she had no idea what would happen and did her best not to think about it. The good Lord would just have to provide and that was that.

Etta left the swimming hole brushing her wet hair out of her eyes, then went to retrieve her clothes. There was one Darling left—Oliver, the youngest. She didn't see much of him as he was always busy with his brothers and had also been sprayed by a skunk some weeks ago. The last time she saw him for any length of time was in this very spot, fishing. Hadn't he walked her back to town? Who was with them? Was it Dora or Jean? She couldn't remember. But it didn't matter, anyway. She'd caught some fish and could eat that night.

Speaking of which, she'd better mind her pole. She slipped into her clothes, enjoying the dampness of her underthings against her skin. They would keep her cool for the rest of the day and into the evening. Maybe she should pick some apples later, then take a walk toward Letty's place. Sterling and Letty were often seen on the road as Sterling went back and forth between Letty's and the hotel where he and the rest of his brothers resided.

She cast her line again. So far, she'd had no luck. She hoped that changed or she'd have to have apples again for dinner.

After an hour she still hadn't gotten a bite, so she gathered her things and decided to try again later. The fish were often biting at dusk. She could eat a late dinner and have an apple for dessert.

She headed up the trail to the small road that would take her back to town. It was a lonely walk, and she always thought of her father. They'd walked to the fishing and swimming spot many times over the years. Then in a blink of an eye, Pa was gone, gunned down by outlaws that robbed the bank.

She licked her dry lips. Memories of what happened always gave her a sour taste in her mouth and she spit just to rid herself of it. Thoughts of what happened that fateful day made her blood boil. The killings were senseless, and if she ever got the chance to face the outlaw that killed her pa, she'd shoot them herself. Pa had his flaws, and some would say he was better off dead, but no one deserved to be shot down like that.

She stopped in the middle of the road. "Forgive me, Lord. Again." She opened her eyes and continued walking. She shouldn't be having such thoughts, but couldn't help it. The pain of her father's murder cut deep, and maybe she should have talked to Letty about it. But Letty had lost her pa and her brother as well. She had enough trouble of her own.

So Etta kept quiet and tried to cope with the loss as best she could. Staying fed was her main concern, and if she could get the roof patched on the livery stable and a few other things repaired, that would be a lot taken off her mind. That is, if the Darlings hadn't forgotten about her. Sometimes she wondered if they remembered who she was. But that was okay. She didn't want to be noticed lest she get herself killed one day too.

Chapter Two

Herbert Coolidge filled his canteen and glared at his younger brother Jonny. "Hurry up, we don't have all day."

Jonny, the youngest of the three Coolidge brothers, scowled at him, then turned to their middle brother Dale. "What's in his craw? He's been uppity all day."

Dale rolled his eyes. "That's because he's worrying about joining up with that Frank Lawson."

Jonny eyed their older brother. He'd gone upstream and was speaking quietly to their cousin Dilbert. "That Lawson fella was with Ted Rush's gang, and we all know what happened to Ted."

"Yeah, he done got caught. I don't fancy decorating a cottonwood, do you?"

"No sirree." Jonny dipped his canteen into the stream. "Does that Lawson fella know we're just starting out?"

"I hope so." Dale looked across the stream to the woods beyond. "Herb says Lawson's somewhere here in the Montana Territory. Says there's more places to hide out there. After what happened to Ted's gang in Clear Creek, he didn't stay in Oregon any longer than he had to. Guess he didn't have much luck in Washington Territory either."

"Why can't we just form our own gang?" Jonny whined.

"Because we ain't got the experience or the manpower," Dale replied. "And we need protection. Frank Lawson's got connections. He can help us get what we need."

"How do we know we can trust him?" Jonny finished filling his canteen and stood.

"We don't," Herbert said, joining them. "But we ain't got much choice. Either we join up with someone who knows what they're doing or we keep doing these small-time jobs and risk getting caught."

The brothers fell into a sullen silence as they gathered their gear and headed back toward their horses. They knew Herbert was right. They had to take a chance and hope Lawson wouldn't lead them astray. But the thought of being part of a gang still made Jonny uneasy. He'd heard stories of what happened when things went wrong and wasn't sure he was ready to trust the likes of a hardened outlaw. But isn't that exactly what they were setting out to become?

They rode for hours, trying to keep to the shade as

much as possible, until they reached a small town. "Looks like we might need to stock up on supplies," Herbert said, looking around at the various stores and saloons.

Dale nodded in agreement. "And maybe we can find out a bit more about this Lawson fella."

They split up, with Herbert and Dilbert heading to the general store and Dale and Jonny going to the saloon for a drink and some information.

Dale ordered a shot of whiskey for himself and one for Jonny, then leaned against the bar. "You hear anything about a fella named Frank Lawson?"

The bartender narrowed his eyes. "Why are you asking?"

"Just curious," Dale said.

The bartender leaned in close. "Word is he's been causing trouble in these parts. Robbing banks and stage-coaches."

Jonny leaned forward eagerly. "Where can we find him?"

The bartender shrugged. "Don't rightly know. But I heard he's got a hideout up in the hills."

Dale finished his whiskey. "Thanks for the information."

As they walked out of the saloon, Jonny turned to Dale. "We don't have to do this, ya know. We can turn back now and forget about joining up with this Lawson fella."

Dale snorted. "And do what? Live out the rest of our

lives as nobodies in some small town? No thanks. I want a taste of the good life, and that means taking risks."

Jonny shifted from foot to foot. "But what about if we get caught?"

His brother smirked. "We won't get caught. Not if we stick together and follow Lawson's lead. He's got the know-how. All we have to do is listen and do what he says."

Jonny sighed, glancing over his shoulder at the saloon. "I don't like it, but I suppose it's better than sitting around doing nothing."

"That's the spirit." Dale grinned. "Now come on, let's go catch up with Herbert and Dilbert and tell 'em what the barkeep said."

The brothers trudged up the street toward the general store, their footsteps heavy with the weight of their decision. They were leaving behind everything they knew, everything they'd ever wanted, in pursuit of something more. Something risky, dangerous, and exciting. But they knew they had no idea what they were getting themselves into.

As they entered the store, the bell above the door jingled. Dilbert was already at the counter, haggling with the owner over the price of a new rifle.

"Hey, we got some information at the saloon," Dale said, approaching his cousin.

Herbert turned from the pair of boots he was examining. "What did ya find out?"

Dale lowered his voice. "Barkeep said that Lawson's

been causing trouble around here, robbing banks and stagecoaches."

Herbert's face split into a grin. "I knew he was our kind of fella. Did ya hear where his hideout is?"

"Up in the hills somewhere."

"Well, that's good enough for me." Herbert slapped his hand on the counter. "Let's stock up on supplies and head out. We've got a gang to join, boys."

On the third day of their search, the sun had begun to set when they reached a small cabin in the woods. Dilbert, who had ridden ahead to scout the area, met them behind a rock outcropping a few hundred feet away. "It's clear," he said to Herbert, who was already dismounting. "And sure enough, someone's inside."

Herbert studied the front door. "If it's Lawson, he's liable to shoot one of us. Best I do the talking."

The four of them crept toward the cabin. Once on the front porch, Herbert burst through the door, a wide grin on his face. "Mr. Lawson?"

Frank Lawson stood up from a table where he was eating, gun drawn. He looked them over, eyes narrowing. "I 'spect you're the Coolidge brothers. I hear tell you've been lookin' for me."

"I don't know how ya heard, but ya heard right." Herbert stepped closer. "And ya know what we want."

Frank laughed and holstered his gun. "You boys sure you want to join up with me?"

Dale stepped forward, puffing out his chest. "We're sure. We're ready for anything."

Frank sneered. "Anythin', huh? From what I hear, you boys don't know the first thing about bein' an outlaw."

"We're willing to learn," Herbert said, his tone steady.

Frank walked over to them, his boots thudding on the wooden floor. "What are your names?"

"I'm Herbert." He gestured to his brothers in turn. "That's Dale, Jonny, and our cousin Dilbert."

Frank nodded. "Well, seein' as how I shot most of my last gang for tryin' to betray me, I could use a few extra hands. Just remember, if *you* ever betray me, I'll kill ya like I killed them."

The Coolidge brothers exchanged a few concerned looks, but said nothing. Besides, this was the famous Frank Lawson! At long last, they were going to be part of a real outlaw gang!

Over the next few weeks, they traveled deeper into Montana Territory and Frank taught them everything he knew about robbing stagecoaches. He showed them how to shoot, how to ride fast and hard, and how to cover their tracks. They practiced until their fingers were numb and their bodies ached, but they never complained. They were living the life they had always dreamed of, and they weren't about to back out now.

One evening, Herbert cornered Frank and asked what the rest wanted to know. "Frank, when are we gonna rob a bank?"

Frank smiled. "Soon enough, and I know just where to go."

"Where's that?"

"Virginia City. They got themselves a fine little bank."

Herbert grinned ear to ear. "Now that's more like it. When do we leave?"

Frank checked his gun. "At first light. Best tell the others."

Herbert, still grinning, went to do just that.

"Phileas, what do you have left to do on the hotel?" Sterling asked.

Phileas launched into his list of tasks as Oliver reached for the mashed potatoes. Once Sterling made his mind up about something, there was little any of them could do to change it. The eldest Darlington had decided that Phileas and Dora should be the ones to return to England and inform their parents that the rest of them were remaining in Apple Blossom. Phileas himself announced the plan when he proposed to Dora not three weeks ago.

But everyone knew Sterling had the final say. He was the next Viscount Darlington. The six of them agreed they would adopt a rotation system, each spending two months in England to see to the estate and the care of their mother once their father passed. It could be years before that happened, but they wanted their plan in place and regardless of how long their father lived, begin their rotations.

Oliver bit into the fried chicken Dora had made. Mr. McSweeney, Captain Stanley's friend, had made the side dishes and desserts. "This is delicious, Dora," Oliver commented between bites.

She smiled at him across the table. "Thank you, Oliver. I hope your parents like my cooking."

Conrad laughed. "Oh dear, I hadn't thought of that." He looked around the table, then over his shoulder at the kitchen door. Mr. McSweeney was putting the finishing touches on his dessert and was thankfully out of earshot. Still, Conrad lowered his voice. "I'm afraid our cook might not let you in the kitchen."

Dora gave him a blank look. "Cook?"

Phileas put his hand over hers. "Yes, dear one. You must remember, we have an entire house staff complete with housekeeper and head butler. But if you'd like to make dinner, I'm sure we can talk Mother into it."

Dora put her hand to her chest. "You mean she has to decide if I can cook or not?"

"Mother is in charge of the household staff. She goes over the menus with our cook daily."

Cassie and Letty exchanged a look of panic. "I never knew so much went into a large household," Letty said.

Oliver laughed. "You'd be surprised. Not that I pay much attention. I'm usually too busy helping Father."

"And he appreciates the help, Ollie," Irving said. "But

we'll have to face facts, everyone. This will upset the household."

Oliver noticed the worried looks of the women. They'd had dinner together, all of them, to discuss their plans.

"When would you like Phileas and me to leave?" Oliver asked.

Sterling drummed his fingers on the tabletop. "In a couple of weeks. I want to get this doctor business straightened out. Does anyone know if Agnes wrote her nephew again?"

"She told me she did last week," Sarah, Irving's betrothed, said.

Oliver glanced at Sarah's children Flint and Lacey and hoped they didn't repeat any of tonight's conversation. No one else in Apple Blossom knew they were from nobility, and they wanted to keep it that way. It was safer for all of them.

"If Agnes' nephew arrives in the next couple of weeks, that would be perfect," Phileas said. "I should have the hotel wrapped up by then."

"Which brings me to the rest of the list," Sterling said. "We have done nothing for poor Etta." He smiled at Letty. "She hasn't brought it up either. Does she still want us to work on her place?"

Letty dabbed her mouth with a napkin. "Etta is quiet and puts others first. She's not one to ask for help, I'm afraid. But of everyone that you've helped so far, she needs it the most."

Jean nodded and put her hand over Wallis'. "If you think my place was small, you should see Etta's. It's just a tiny room in the back of the livery stable, barely big enough for a cot and a small dresser."

Oliver's eyes widened. "What?" He'd inspected the livery stable and blacksmith shop not long after they arrived in Apple Blossom. He didn't remember a room with a bed and dresser. Had he skipped it accidentally? "Where is it?"

"Just off the shop. It's where Etta and her father slept until she got older."

Everyone's jaws dropped. "You've got to be joking," Irving said.

Letty shook her head. "I'm afraid not. They slept with their cots pushed together—that way they still had room for the dresser."

Wallis's eyes widened. "I say, poor Etta must have been treated like a son instead of a daughter."

Dora shrugged. "Silas Whitehead was, shall we say, unconventional? But he raised Etta as best he could. He just never thought to build a house to live in."

"That poor girl," Sterling said. "Well, chaps, looks like we have our work cut out for us. We'll need building supplies, and a floor plan of course, and stone for a fireplace..."

Oliver swallowed his mashed potatoes. "Brother, are you thinking of building her a cabin?"

"I am. I'm sure we can put one up."

"But that could take weeks, months!" Oliver protested.

"It will take *us* weeks or months," Conrad pointed out. "You'll be off to England with Phileas and Dora."

Oliver tapped his fork on his plate. "I should have seen such a room, but I can't recall it."

"That Etta slept in a drafty storeroom?" Dora glanced at Jean. "So did Jean for a number of years, and no one thought anything of it. It's just the way life was here."

"And then you six came along," Sarah said. "And look what you've done for us. Our gratitude isn't enough. And poor Etta—once you've built a little cabin for her, I don't know what she'll do."

"A simple thank you is enough," Sterling said. "Your town needed help, and we could give it. Right, brothers?"

The rest nodded and got back to eating.

When the meal was finished Mr. McSweeney hurried out with an elaborate cake that would make their cook back home green with envy. "I think I've outdone myself," he said. "I hope you all like it. I also hope I put enough lemon into the batter. I bought Alma out."

Everyone gawked at the fancy confection. "My word, McSweeney," Oliver said. "It's magnificent!" He licked his lips, then looked for a knife to cut the cake.

"It is, isn't it?" McSweeney said proudly. He produced a knife from his back pocket. "Allow me."

Oliver waited in anticipation with the rest of them as Mr. McSweeney sliced the cake. He had a fleeting thought of taking some to Etta, but then it was gone. Maybe she didn't want charity. But the more he thought about her living situation, the more it irked him. How could he have missed it? And what about the rest of them? They'd all been so busy helping the other women in town that somehow Etta got brushed aside.

"Oliver," Sterling said. "There's no need to feel guilty."

He swallowed when he realized he was wearing his heart on his sleeve. "I know, it's just that I feel bad. I should have put two and two together. We could have helped her first."

Letty glanced at the others. "Now I feel guilty."

Sterling cupped her face in his hand. "Don't. None of us knew and Etta never complained. We'll take care of it and build her a cabin so she has a decent place to live. There's plenty of room for one behind the livery."

Letty put her hand over his and smiled. "Thank you. I know she'll love it."

Sterling nodded, turned to Oliver and grinned. "I want you to tell Etta first thing in the morning."

Chapter Three

E tta fitted the shoe to Mr. Watson's horse Clyde, pulled a nail from her mouth, and hammered it into place. Once again, she thought about her future and how long she'd be able to keep the blacksmith shop operating. She supposed once Apple Blossom started growing, she could sell the shop and do something else. But she loved her work, hard though it was, and she loved horses.

She finished with the gelding's right front hoof, ducked under the horse's neck and lifted the left front leg. "Ready for the next?"

Clyde looked at her, then flicked an ear toward her.

She smiled as she got to work, heard a noise and looked up. "Who's there?"

Oliver Darling entered the shop, hands up as if she held a gun on him. "It's only me. I didn't mean to startle you. Please accept my most humble apology."

She fought the urge to roll her eyes. The Darlings were more than polite and she didn't know how to act around them. "That's all right. What do you want?" She put Clyde's leg down and straightened, wiping hair from her eyes. "Do you need your horse saddled?"

"No, I need you... I mean... well, we want to work on your place."

She smiled as his cheeks went bright red. "Oh?"

He pulled at his collar. Why was he so nervous? "Yes, Sterling has decided that it's time. If you'll excuse me a moment?" He glanced at the door on the far wall, then headed straight for it.

"What are you doing?" she cried as she followed. "That's my private space."

He looked at her when he reached it. "I'm aware. But I still want to see it."

She maneuvered around him to stand in front of the door. "Why?"

"I want to see how much space you have."

She laughed.

Oliver eased her aside. "Please, we're only trying to help."

"Fine, but I don't know how much help you can give that room other than to patch the walls."

He smiled warmly, opened the door and gasped. "My word, woman. This is where you sleep?" His voice cracked on the last word.

Her shoulders slumped. What must he think of her now? She knew she had the smallest living space in town, or second only to Jean. But at least Jean's place resembled a home. Hers was just a storeroom. Well, more like a closet...

Oliver slowly backed out of the room. "You poor thing."

"Stop right there," she said, pointing at him. "This might be all we have, but we were proud of it, my father and I."

He smiled again. "I daresay, young lady, that yes, you were. You have this livery stable and a fine blacksmith's shop. But what you don't have are decent living quarters." He re-entered the room, went straight to the far wall, and stuck his finger through a knothole. "How do you stay warm at night?"

She shrugged. "The forge. Sometimes I leave the door open." She noticed the softness of her voice and winced. She wasn't that embarrassed by it. It could be worse.

Oliver gave her a look that said it couldn't. "We're going to build you a cabin."

Her jaw dropped. "A what?"

"Sterling and the rest of us have decided." He left the small room and joined her. "I'll need to look out back. I'm sure there's plenty of room."

She gulped. "But the orchards are out back. There's a clearing but ..."

He looked into her eyes. "It will do." He left the blacksmith shop.

Etta looked at Clyde. "I'll be right back." She darted out after the man. "Oliver! Wait!" She caught up to him in the small clearing. There *was* room for a cabin. Even a full-sized house. "You can't," she blurted.

He walked a wide circle, eyeing the clearing, probably measuring in his head. "Can't what?"

"Build me a cabin."

Oliver stopped and looked at her. "Good heavens, why not?"

"Because it wouldn't be fair."

He slowly approached. "What do you mean?"

Without thinking she backed up a step. "To the others, I mean. Letty, Sarah, Jean, Dora and Cassie."

Oliver shook his head. "I'm sorry, but I'm afraid I don't understand. How is it not fair?"

"Because you didn't build them new houses. You only repaired what they had." She turned away. "It's too much."

She felt a warm hand on her shoulder as Oliver turned her to face him. "Etta, how is helping you any different? You live in... well, something unlivable. You need a home. Four walls that are bigger than what you have and not full of knotholes."

Tears stung her eyes, and she didn't know why. Oh drat, drat, drat! Why was this upsetting her so? "It's too much," she repeated.

"It's not enough," he shot back. "How long have you lived like this? What of your mother?"

She swallowed hard. "My mother has been gone a long time. When Pa and I moved here it was just the two of us."

He gave her a hard stare and she could just imagine what was going through his head. "And your father never provided a decent home?"

She shrugged. "What we had was enough."

He looked at the back of the shop and livery stable. "You slept on a cot in that tiny room with your father?"

She shook her head. "When I was young. Pa took to sleeping in one of the stalls when I got older. He said it wasn't proper for us to be crammed into that small space together. I needed my privacy."

He rubbed his face with his hands and looked at her again. "My dear woman, we will do this for you, and will brook no argument. You will have a decent place to live, is that understood?"

She gaped at him. "Are you telling me what to do?"

"No, I'm telling you what *we're* going to do." He closed the distance between them and looked down at her. She hadn't been this close to one of the Darlings before. "One bedroom or two?"

"What?"

"Would you like one bedroom or two?"

She shook her head in disbelief. She thought they'd patch a few holes, repair the roof, but not this! "I … I don't know."

"Two, then." He turned around and looked at the clearing. "In fact, we could make it a two-story cottage. Phileas can draw up the plans—he's good at that sort of thing." He stepped into the middle of the clearing. "The parlor can go here. We could put the dining room across the hall and the staircase in the center. And in the back would be an enormous kitchen running the length of the house." He looked at her and smiled. "That way you can use the dining room for formal entertaining."

Etta gaped at him. "What?"

He moved forward about twenty feet. "Imagine the front door here." He looked at her and grinned, then turned on his heel. "The center staircase here with banisters on both sides so you can see through the parlor to the dining room." He took big steps as if he was taking two stairs at a time. "Up here is the landing, with a lovely center window overlooking the orchards behind the house." He turned to his right. "We'll have one bedroom here." He turned to the left. "And the other bedroom there. You could use it for a sewing room or whatnot." He faced her and took rapid steps as if running down the staircase, then made as if he was opening the front door, stepped out and closed it. "Over here," he said and pointed to his right, "you could have a small garden." He walked around the imaginary house and headed to the back.

Etta followed, fascinated by his behavior. Had he gone 'round the bend?

Oliver walked the length of the imaginary house. "See? You have plenty of room in the back for a picnic area. And we'll put in a back door for the kitchen and maybe a little back porch. Then you can sit out here in the evening and admire the orchards. True, it will be a cabin of sorts but we could still paint it white and add some green shutters, I think... and you could even have a picket fence if you'd like. For the children, of course. I imagine you'll have some one day." He faced her. "How does that sound?"

Etta continued to gawk. "I ... I don't think it can be done."

Oliver closed the distance between them. "On the contrary, Etta Whitehead. We've already begun."

Oliver stared at Etta's horrified expression. "You needn't worry," he assured her, but she didn't look convinced. He tried not to fidget and stepped back, putting some distance between them.

She put her hand to her temple. "I can't accept."

He cocked his head in confusion. "Why not? We've helped your friends and none of them argued. They welcomed the aid."

"Yes, I know, but this is more than patching a few holes. I can't let you build me a house. I'll never be able to repay you."

His chest tightened. She was scared, he could see it in her eyes. "You don't have to," he said gently. He didn't want to upset her any more than she already was.

Etta paced. "Everything you described is wonderful. Beautiful, even. I can see it in my head. But it will take too long and..."

"The house would be done before winter, Etta. We'll

put a fireplace in the parlor, and we could even put a small one in the kitchen at one end. The cookstove could be at the other. If we build it properly, the heat will rise and warm the upstairs bedrooms through grates."

She stared at him, wide-eyed. If Oliver didn't know any better he'd say she was about to cry. But he wasn't sure they'd be happy tears. She looked nervous, upset. "Etta, we're going to help you. We apologize it's taken so long..."

She held up a hand, shaking her head. "It's not that. It's just ..." She pinched the bridge of her nose. "I don't take kindly to charity. Neither did Pa."

"Don't think of it as charity. It's a gift."

She wrung her hands. "A costly one. Don't you understand? How can you afford to build me a house? I can see a few pieces of furniture, paint, wallpaper." She pointed toward the hotel. "Your brother must have spent a fortune on Dora's place."

He looked toward Phileas' masterpiece. He couldn't see it from where they were standing, but knew what had been done. The hotel was gorgeous, and still not finished, though Phileas was getting close.

"You're leaving."

He turned to her. "For a time." He looked at the ground. Was it a lie? Would he be back? Phileas and Dora would return, but he couldn't say the same for himself.

"What's the matter?" she asked. "*Are* you coming back?"

Great, the question was for him and him alone. "I'm not sure about myself. But Phileas and Dora will return."

"And then what?" she asked. "Are the others leaving for England too?"

"No. My brothers want to stay. But we do need to let our parents know what's going on. And we need to be there for them as they age. That's why we're going to rotate."

She stared at him a moment. "You'll take turns going to England?"

"That's right. Phileas, Dora and I will go first, inform our parents of our brothers' wives, stay a while to help out, then come back. After that, Sterling and Letty will go."

"And who will take care of Letty's place when they do?"

"We'll all pitch in. We're not worried about it, Etta. You shouldn't be either. It's not your problem. What is," he said and pointed at the livery stable, "is that sorry excuse for a shelter."

She gasped.

Oliver fought the urge to roll his eyes. "I apologize. That was uncalled for and not very nice."

"I think you've said enough. Now go away." She turned on her heel and marched back toward the blacksmith's shop.

"Etta..." He started after her.

"What?" She stopped short.

"You're taking this all wrong." He put a hand on her

shoulder, turning her around. "Think about it. When will you get another chance like this? We're offering to build you a house."

Her hand flew to her chest. "That's just it. Why would you do such a thing?" She turned and began walking again.

Oliver had to trot to keep up with her. "I don't understand what the problem is."

She spun around so fast he almost bumped into her. "I'll tell you what the problem is. When people are this nice, there's something wrong. You aren't doing this for nothing." She hugged herself and backed away.

Oliver's eyes widened. "What happened?" he heard himself ask. "I mean, I don't want to pry, but I don't understand you."

She closed her eyes a moment and let her arms drop. "There's nothing to understand. I'm sorry. I'm... upset, surprised. People just don't go around offering to build other people's houses. Not for free."

"We'll all pitch in. And I'm sure there will be donations..."

She covered her face with her hands and groaned.

"People donated things for the library," he continued.

Her hands slid down her face. "It's bad enough everyone in this town thinks I'm a charity case. But I ask nothing from them. Nothing!"

Oliver stood flummoxed. What was wrong with her? What had happened? "It's all right," he said softly.

"We're offering to help and expect nothing in return. You're part of this town and you deserve to be treated the same as everyone else. Why wouldn't that be so?"

She swallowed hard. "Because my pa... he... wasn't nice at times."

Oliver straightened as he looked at her. "What do you mean?"

Etta scratched the back of her neck and looked away. "He drank. And when he did, he got mean."

"Did he hurt you?"

She shook her head. "But he threatened to hurt others sometimes. I was afraid he'd lose business. Some folks would bring their horses to be shod and have me do it. He alienated half the town before he died." She hugged herself again.

Oliver nodded in understanding. "He made you a pariah."

She looked at him with narrowed eyes. "What does that mean?"

He slowly closed the distance between them. "An outcast. But I don't think that's the case now. True, your father is gone and I'm sorry, we all are. But that doesn't mean you don't deserve a decent roof over your head. Understand?" He hoped he wasn't making a mess of this. Maybe Sterling should have sent Irving or Phileas. They were good with words.

Etta shook her head. "I'm sorry. I just don't know what to think. No one's ever offered anything so generous."

"Perhaps it's because no one had the means to. But there are six of us, and when we pull together, we can do quite a lot in a short amount of time. Even after Phileas, Dora, and I leave for England, you'll still have four of us to help. Besides, we're all quite convincing when we want to be. I'm sure we can coerce some of the locals into helping as well."

She scoffed. "I hope so. I can just imagine the look on Agnes' face when she finds out. She'll say that the land doesn't belong to me and want to sell it."

He looked around. "Does this belong to you?"

She nodded. "Livery stable, blacksmith's shop, and about an acre of land behind it. The entire clearing and part of the orchard."

"Well then, there's nothing she can do about it, is there?"

"I hope not. Agnes likes to get her hands into everybody's business and take what she can."

Oliver's eyes narrowed. "Has she always been like that?"

Etta closed her own eyes and shook her head. "You have no idea."

Chapter Four

Etta finished shoeing Mr. Atkins' horse, then grabbed her fishing pole and left the shop. She needed to be alone to think about all that Oliver had said. Would his offer cause her more trouble? She kept out of trouble by staying quiet, keeping to herself, not complaining about her lot in life. Pa at least had taught her that much. Probably because he'd learned to do the same after he'd been drinking.

She made her way to the creek, preoccupied with Oliver's proposal. She wondered if it was worth it, to risk everything she'd built for herself in this small town. Not only would Agnes complain she got a house for free but would stick her nose into every corner of her business. Thank the Lord she owned the blacksmith's shop and livery stable, or the woman would try to figure out a way to foreclose on her, even if she was up to date on her payments.

When she reached the fishing hole, she hiked upstream, sat on a rock and cast her line into the water. The breeze rustling the leaves and the sound of the rushing creek helped to soothe her nerves. If she were smart, she'd take the offer Oliver and his brothers gave her and be done with it. But Pa said no one gave something for nothing, especially men. She gulped at the thought and waited for a fish to bite.

She took a shuddering breath as her thoughts drifted back to her past. Growing up the way she had made her tough, but it also made her wary of trust. She'd learned to rely on herself and no one else. But Oliver had broken through her protective walls with his charm and kindness. Drat the man! And those eyes of his, so warm and inviting. Did he have to be so handsome? Ugh!

Etta felt a tug on her line and quickly pulled up a fish. She smiled to herself, feeling a small sense of accomplishment. Maybe Oliver's offer was worth the risk after all.

As she continued to fish, she planned out her next steps. She would have to be cautious, but she was confident in her ability to handle whatever came her way. If the Darlings' offer was legitimate and Oliver wasn't speaking out of turn, then she'd speak to Sterling. He was the leader of the six and would confirm everything Oliver said. From the sounds of it, this was Sterling's idea.

She smiled as she remembered the way Oliver walked through her future house, pointing everything out but the furniture.

She groaned. "I don't have any. How will I get some?" She tried not to think about it as she continued to fish. She would catch what she could and eat it tonight.

She supposed having a nice cookstove would make life easier. And what did he say about a second fireplace in the kitchen? That would be nice too. With grates placed just right, the upstairs bedrooms would have heat in the winter. Maybe she could have Letty help her decorate...

She pushed the thought aside, pulled in her line and left the rock. She needed to return to town.

Thank goodness she hadn't been gone long. The last thing she needed was for Agnes to wander into the blacksmith's shop, see she was gone, then run to Mr. Featherstone and complain. Still, on her way back to town, she had a renewed sense of determination. She would take Oliver's offer and build a better life for herself. She was tired of living in fear, always looking over her shoulder, jumping at every sound. She was ready for a change.

As she walked down Apple Blossom's main street, her excitement built. She was going to have her own house, and with it her own sense of freedom. No longer would she have to worry about people pitying her or Agnes' constant meddling. She could finally breathe easy. Maybe she could make some extra money and pay the Darlings back for their kindness. An entire house was no small feat, and it wasn't cheap either. She'd have to figure something out and quick.

Etta was so deep in thought, she didn't notice Agnes sitting outside the shop, waiting for her. Her heart sank when she did see her, but she kept her composure—and her excitement hidden.

"Where have you been?" Agnes asked, her voice dripping with suspicion.

"Just out for a walk." Etta tried to sound nonchalant as she put her hand with the fish behind her back. "Is there something you needed?"

Agnes huffed. "I was wondering when you were going to finish the repairs on my buggy."

Etta bit her lip. She'd been working on the buggy, but it wasn't a priority. After all, it wasn't as if the Featherstones had any place to go. Besides, she'd had other things on her mind, and now had Oliver's offer and her future home to think about. If she tried to explain this to Agnes, she'd have none of it.

As if listening to her thoughts, Agnes said, "You need to focus on this shop, girl. If you can't handle it, maybe you should find a different line of work."

Etta stiffened. She'd worked hard to build up her business, and she wasn't about to let Agnes tear it down. She took a deep breath. "I'll have your buggy ready tomorrow."

Agnes looked her up and down. "Very well." She left the bench and headed for the street. "And clean that fish and bury the guts or your place will stink more than it does."

Etta sighed as Agnes stomped off, then looked at the

fish she held. She went into the shop, grabbed a small knife, then went out back to gut her fish. After her lunch, she'd find Sterling and see what he had to say. She could feel her heart pounding just thinking about speaking with him and tried to ignore it.

As she worked on the fish, she tried to imagine what life would be like in the house the Darlings planned to build. She'd worked so hard to build the business and make a life for herself in this town, even before Pa was killed. People respected her work, and dare she say her? Yes, Pa made life difficult, and folks looked down on them for years. Would they look down on her again if she let the Darlings build her a home? Would some folks be jealous?

But as she thought about it more, she once again realized she was tired of just surviving. She wanted to thrive. And maybe, just maybe, this was her chance. If the town grew, and more and more folks moved to Apple Blossom, would her pretty little house behind the livery stable say something about her?

She thought about it throughout her meal and, after finishing her lunch, set out to find Sterling. She had a feeling where he would be today, and headed for the hotel. As she walked, her earlier sense of excitement pooled in her chest. It had to be a good sign.

When she finally found him, he was in the back of the hotel, chatting with some of his brothers. She took a deep breath and approached. "Mr. Darling?" she said tentatively. Should she have addressed him by his Christian name? She did his brothers.

Sterling turned to look at her, his expression neutral. "Yes, Etta? What can I do for you?"

She clasped her hands before her and tried to keep her nerves under control. "I wanted to speak with you about the offer your brother made me."

Sterling raised an eyebrow. "What about it?"

Etta took a deep breath. "I think I want to accept it."

Sterling's expression softened. "I see. And why the change of heart? Oliver told me it sounded like you wanted nothing to do with it."

Etta hesitated. She wasn't sure if she should say anything about Pa and what it was like growing up with someone whom many considered the town drunk. "I was taken by surprise, that's all."

He smiled. "We only want to help."

She swallowed hard. "Then... I..." Another deep breath. "... accept."

Agnes marched into the bank, went to her desk and sat. She straightened a few papers, lined up her pencils, dipped her pen in the inkwell and wrote. *Etta White-head, owner of the Apple Blossom livery stable and blacksmith's shop, is hereby deemed ineligible for any loan from this establishment.* She blew on the ink to dry it, then continued to write. *Furthermore, it has come to the bank's attention that Miss Whitehead's character further excludes her from this bank's services. If her misguided ways are not corrected, she will no longer be a customer of this bank.*

She blew on the ink some more, then smiled in satisfaction. Etta had always been easy to control, and she wasn't about to lose that control now. If it weren't for those darn Darlings coming to town, things would be just as they'd always been since the incident.

Agnes' eyes darted around the bank. Francis was in his office doing who knew what while Mr. Miller busied himself at the teller's station with Mrs. Smythe. Hmmm, where was Mr. Smythe? And what about Mr. and Mrs. Atkins? Didn't they usually come to town on Thursdays?

She straightened in her chair. She hated when things weren't on schedule. And what had Oliver Darling been doing at the blacksmith's shop earlier? She hadn't seen him ride out, so what business did he have there? Was there something wrong with his horse? She should have asked Etta while she was there but had to return to the bank, then home to fix Francis his lunch. She hoped he wasn't sneaking a snooze about now. She turned and eyed the door to his office. Hmmm, should she find out?

She was about to when Sterling Darling and his younger brother Oliver walked into the bank. Now what did they want? She stood. "Can I help you?"

"Yes," Sterling said. "I'd like to open an account."

She gaped at him. "You?"

"What's wrong with that? I plan to live here."

She snapped her mouth shut, then looked at his younger brother. "And what about you?"

He stuck his hands in his pockets. "I'm going home soon. There's no point, is there?"

She glanced between them. She'd like to see them all go home. They were a disruption to her usual routine, and she was done with it.

"Mrs. Featherstone?" Sterling prompted. "My account?"

Her eyes narrowed. "Do you have any money?"

He smiled. "If I didn't, would I be here?"

She blushed with embarrassment. There was no need to make a fool of herself. "Very well." She sat and pulled the paperwork from a drawer in her desk. "Just fill these out."

He sat at a chair on the other side of the desk and perused the papers. "Might I have a pen?"

She rolled her eyes impatiently and shoved the inkwell and pen across the desk.

He smiled again and began to fill out the papers. The younger Darling fidgeted, and she wondered what he was so nervous about. "What were you doing at the livery stable earlier? Something wrong with your horse?"

He froze and stared at her, then looked at his brother. "N-nothing. Just spoke with Etta."

"Miss Whitehead probably had little to say. She never does." She peeked at the paperwork to see how far the older Darling had gotten. "Hurry it up, I haven't got all day."

Sterling looked at her, set the pen down, then slowly turned the first page over and started filling out the second.

Agnes frowned deeper. He did that on purpose! The lout! She had a right mind to refuse him an account. "What will you be depositing?"

"You mean how much?"

Oliver smiled. "I believe she knows it's money, brother."

Agnes fumed. How dare they make fun of her! "Of course I meant money," she snapped. "How much?"

Sterling reached into the inside pocket of his jacket and pulled out a billfold. "Let's see, three hundred dollars ought to be enough."

Her eyes widened at the sight of the money. "Three hundred? Where did you get that kind of money?"

"Come now, Mrs. Featherstone, it's not all that much."

Her eyes narrowed again. "It is to some around here."

"Who?" Oliver asked.

Was he being impertinent? "If you haven't figured that out by now, then I doubt you ever will."

"Are you talking about Etta?" Oliver asked.

"Why bring her up?"

He leaned against the desk. "She sleeps in a room no bigger than a butler's pantry. In fact, I imagine its smaller than some pantries."

"And how would you know how big a butler's pantry is?"

"Do you have one?" he shot back.

"Ollie, that's enough." Sterling finished the second sheet then shoved it back across the desk along with the pen and inkwell. "There, all done." He pulled the money out of his billfold and slid that to her too.

"Aren't you afraid the bank will be robbed?" she asked.

"Will it?"

Her eyes flicked to Mr. Miller and back. "Of course not." She scooped up the money and paperwork, and headed for the teller. "Here. Mr. Darling is opening an account."

Mr. Miller removed his spectacles. "He is? How wonderful." He took everything from her and went to open the safe.

Agnes saw nothing wonderful about it. She wanted nothing more than to be rid of Sterling Darling and his brothers. The sooner the better, as far as she was concerned. They were ruining her little utopia, and she hoped when her nephew Reuben arrived and took over the doctoring, they'd leave. But the oldest was staying. What about the others? Soon she'd lose control over the town and folks would stop listening to her. What a horrible thought!

"What about the others?" Oliver asked. "Will they be opening accounts too?"

"Eventually," Sterling said. "But there are things that

need to happen first. Phileas will take care of all of that when he goes home."

Oliver nodded in understanding and stepped away from the desk.

"What do you mean?" Agnes asked. She was being more than a little nosy but didn't care. "Don't tell me you're all planning to stay?"

"We thought it was common knowledge." Sterling stood.

Her hand flew to her chest. It was just as she'd feared! These do-gooders were ruining everything she'd built up! "But you can't stay. None of you are married. I'll not have this town's reputation sullied!"

Sterling smiled. "Fear not, Mrs. Featherstone. If we must, we'll all travel to Virginia City and get married there. It will take a little more time to arrange, but we're willing to do it."

"And if that rabble-rousing captain can muster up a preacher?"

"Then wouldn't it be grand for him to perform a big wedding for all of us? It would be the first of its kind in this town and, I dare say, give everyone something to talk about for years to come."

Oliver smiled and she swore she caught him smirking. Well, at least she'd be rid of *him*. "It could be years before we ever get a preacher. But I'm sure my nephew can take the job once he gets here. He's very well versed in Scripture."

"Is he?" Sterling drawled. "That's an awful lot to ask

of one man. I think the captain should continue his search for a preacher all the same."

She harrumphed and sat. "Well, is there something else? I'm busy."

"No, Mrs. Featherstone. We're leaving now."

"Sterling, the other thing?" Oliver prompted.

"What other thing?" she asked.

"Oh, yes. We'd also like to deposit some money into Etta Whitehead's account."

Her eyes popped wide. "What?"

"Let's see, two hundred dollars, I think. Oliver?"

The younger Darling pulled some money out of his jacket. "Can you see to it?"

She tried not to snarl. "What is it for?"

Oliver smiled. "We're building her a house."

Chapter Five

Oliver and Sterling left the bank in high spirits. "I thought she was going to faint when we deposited that money into Etta's account."

"I thought she might shoot us," Sterling said. "I don't understand why Mrs. Featherstone would be so difficult. It's money and that's what a bank is for. One would think she didn't want ours."

"Maybe she doesn't," Oliver pointed out. "She was rude and mean about it. We're only trying to help, after all. Maybe we should have insisted on dealing with Mr. Featherstone instead."

"Agnes would have found out eventually and probably have made just as big a fuss. Only poor Mr. Featherstone would have taken the brunt. It's better we did things this way. We don't have to live with her."

Oliver laughed. "True, but I hope she doesn't cause

Etta any grief. The poor woman has been through enough from the sound of it. She doesn't need to have Agnes badgering her because of our kindness."

"Yes," Sterling agreed. "And I imagine that's exactly what dear Agnes will do. She likes control, just like Mother, and might be the type to stop at nothing to keep it."

"Then she'd be exactly like Mother." Oliver shuddered at the thought. Their mother drove them crazy but at least she had it in her head that what she was doing was in their best interests. For Agnes Featherstone, he wasn't so sure.

They returned to the hotel and entered the lobby, where Phileas was speaking to Dora and Irving. "Well," Dora said. "Did you do it?"

"Yes." Sterling approached the counter and leaned against it. "Now there's money in Etta's account. She can buy whatever she needs to furnish the house once we finish it. We'll take care of the rest of the cost."

"What will your parents say?" she asked.

Phileas took her hand and kissed it. "The same thing they'll say when they find out I've spent my money on this hotel." The brothers looked at each other then smiled. "You idiots!" they said at once. "What were you thinking?!"

Everyone laughed. "Really?" Dora said. "They'd deem you idiots for helping us out?"

"No, only for spending our money to do it." Oliver

glanced at his brothers. "Well, their money. I haven't spent any of mine yet."

Irving put an arm around him. "But you will. We're all pitching in to take care of Etta's new place. Our tenants live like kings compared to her. It's not right."

"Is her business so bad she couldn't have taken out a loan?" Sterling asked no one in particular.

"She never asked for one, as far as I know," Dora said. "Remember, Etta rarely asks anyone for anything. I know she struggles but as she doesn't complain, she gets overlooked. I'm just as guilty of doing so as everyone else in town."

"She's ashamed," Oliver said. "You can see it in her eyes."

Sterling glanced at Irving and back. "Then perhaps, little brother, what she needs is a friend." He looked at Dora. "No offense, but you won't be working on Etta's house."

"None taken. We were all so wrapped up in our own grief after the incident that people like Sarah and Etta slipped through the cracks. Letty spoke to her the most afterwards, but never said what they talked about. I only spoke to her when I saw her at church. When she went."

"She doesn't always go?" Oliver asked.

Dora shook her head. "She goes to Billy's fishing hole a lot. Maybe because her pa and her used to fish all the time."

"Feeding themselves?" Sterling asked.

Dora's cheeks went pink. "I believe so."

"How could you know?" Phileas said. "Don't start blaming yourself for not doing more."

She blushed a deep pink. "I'm not the only one."

"Going forward, people can start doing more for each other," Sterling said. "Everyone needs to look out for their neighbors."

"Right you are," Oliver said. He stared at the floor. Hadn't Father taught them that very thing by having them help repair their tenants' houses over the years? They'd also helped in the village and repaired the church as well. People were grateful and showed their appreciation in whatever way they could. But a well-run estate meant profit, so of course they were willing to help out and see that the estate ran smoothly. "I should speak to her," he said without thinking.

"And tell her what?" Phileas asked.

Oliver took in the curious gazes of the others. "That her house will be built just as I described it, no surprises, and that she can furnish it as she wishes, and should speak to Alma about it."

"Oliver," Dora said. "Be easy on her if she balks. Etta doesn't think she's worthy of such generosity. I suspect she'll fight you here and there."

"She doesn't trust us, does she?" Irving asked.

"No." Dora sighed. "Give her time."

"Well, I've already sketched out the plans," Phileas said. "I think Oliver's idea of the layout is genius."

He shrugged. "It all popped into my head. I don't know how I saw it so clearly, but I did."

"It's going to look wonderful," Sterling said. "And should be easy to build. Conrad and I will ride out to Mr. Atkins' place tomorrow and speak to him about the lumber we'll need. Then we'll dig the root cellar and measure out the foundation."

"Jolly good," Phileas said. "I'll finish up a few things here while you're doing that, then I can lend a hand."

Sterling nodded and smiled. "Oliver, why don't you let Etta know what we've got planned?"

"Why do I have to do it?"

Irving put an arm around him. "Because you're leaving, and don't you want to return home knowing you've helped in every way you can?"

He took in the expectant looks of his brothers. Even Dora wore one. "Um, okay."

Phileas turned him toward the hotel doors. "Wonderful, off you go." He ushered him across the lobby and opened the door for him. "Be sure to tell her to speak to Alma about the furniture. I hear she wants to carry some in her store."

Oliver nodded as his brother shoved him out the door, then quickly closed it behind him. Was he afraid he'd run back inside?

Oliver straightened his jacket, then marched down the street to the blacksmith's shop. Every time he mentioned what he and his brothers wanted to do, Etta got upset. And when she showed up yesterday to inform Sterling that she'd take them up on their offer, she was still nervous. But at least she said yes. Would she hold to her decision, or tell them no at the last minute? If she did, would they have to sit her down and convince her that letting them build her a little house was the right thing to do?

He stopped before he crossed the street and stared at the blacksmith's shop. What happened that made her so distrusting of others? Had her father made their lives miserable by doing and saying things he shouldn't? Did no one in town think to reach out to Etta and offer help, or was it as Dora said and they were all too wrapped up in their own grief to notice Etta's pain? She lost her father as some others, but from the sounds of it, lost the town's respect long before then. What could he do about it?

Oliver sighed, squared his shoulders and continued across the street.

Etta saw Oliver approaching and frowned. She didn't want to talk to him. In fact, she felt little like talking to anyone now. He would bring up the house and part of her would become overwhelmed while the other part would... well, both parts would be taken aback by the prospect of such kindness. What did they want in return? There had to be something. People weren't that kind and generous. Not to her.

"Etta, there you are," Oliver greeted as he entered the shop. He took off his hat and ran his hand through his hair. "I've come to talk to you."

She was sweeping up bits and pieces of debris from shoeing Mr. Atkins horse earlier. "What?"

He looked into her eyes but said nothing. She supposed he had nice eyes. She stepped closer. Yes, blue, clear, intelligent eyes. And, she noted for the first time, genuine kindness within their depths. Hmmm, maybe their offer was legitimate after all.

"We'll be starting on your house soon and wanted to let you know that you needn't worry about furnishing it."

Her jaw dropped.

His eyebrows shot up and he looked panicked. "Now before you say anything, we've taken care of it."

Her eyes popped wide.

He cringed. "It's a... a gift, from all of us. You'll need things and we wanted you to get them when you wanted."

Her eyes roamed over him. "What did you do?"

He gulped. "We deposited some funds into your bank account."

She sucked in a breath. "You did what?!" Oh no! "Was Agnes there?"

"She helped us, yes."

Etta closed her eyes. She could just imagine what Agnes was thinking. She didn't like anyone disrupting her way of doing things and the Darlings had been doing plenty of it since they arrived in town.

"Etta?" he breathed. "Are you quite all right?"

She sighed. "No." She went to a small bench in the

corner and sat. "Agnes will complain to me about all of you every chance she gets."

He came to the bench and sat. "Why?"

She gave him a sidelong glance and sighed again. "Because that's Agnes for you."

"Hmmm, she likes everyone to be as miserable as she is?" He chuckled. "I dare say, if everyone in town went around wearing the same pinched expression she does, no one will want to settle here."

She snorted. "Indeed, not."

He smiled. "Is she really that bad?"

Etta nodded. "Oh, yes. And you're right, she is miserable and thinks the rest of us should be too." She kicked at some straw on the dusty ground. "I... don't know what to say about the house and the floor plan you're making."

He smiled again. "Not me. Phileas oversees drawing them up. But he did like the ideas I had for it."

She gave him another glance. "They were good ideas."

He grinned. "You really think so?"

She nodded. "I especially like the open staircase separating the parlor and dining room. But the kitchen... what a grand room that will be." She turned to him. "Can you really build such a house?"

"Of course, it should be simple enough. We've done it before."

She searched his face for any sign of ill intent but found none. "And you want nothing in return?"

Their eyes locked. "No, Etta. Nothing. And you don't need to ask again, understand?"

Her heart stilled when she saw the sincerity in his eyes. "Thank you," she whispered.

"Of course." He drew in a breath and looked away. "You're welcome."

She got to her feet. "I should get back to work." Her eyes skipped around the shop. She'd already finished straightening up. She should check on the horses, then try to catch something for dinner. Then again, Mr. Atkins paid her for his horse. She could go to Alma's and buy some beans.

"Can I help you with anything?"

She started. "What?"

Oliver smiled again. "Do you need help with anything while I'm here?"

She stared at him, unable to answer for a moment. No one had offered to help her before. "I... no. I'm fine."

He glanced around the shop. "I must say, this is the tidiest blacksmith's shop I've ever seen."

Her cheeks heated. "Thank you."

"You should join us for dinner tonight."

Her breath hitched. "Dinner?"

"Yes, Mr. McSweeney is cooking. Tonight's supposed to be a surprise. No one knows what he's preparing. We can discuss your house." He tacked on a smile as if that would push her into saying yes.

She thought a moment. Eating something other than fish or beans would be nice. The mere thought made her mouth water. "Well, I wouldn't want to impose..."

"Not at all. Sterling and the others would be happy to have you."

She looked at the dirt floor. "Will Letty be there?"

"I believe so, yes." He smiled again.

She was about to comment when they heard a noise outside. "Horses?" She went to the wide entrance of the shop just as a rider appeared. He rode by at a trot, followed by another rider, then a third. She sucked in a breath. "Strangers."

Oliver went to her side and put a hand on her shoulder. "Steady on. We don't know if they're bad."

She shook, unable to help herself. "They're strangers."

"Hey, it's all right." He turned her to face him. "We were strangers too, remember?"

She backed away so she could peek out of the shop and see where the riders had stopped. All of them were dismounting in front of the saloon. "Where's the captain?"

"I'll find out."

She grabbed his arm as he left. "What if he's not there to serve them? What if they get angry?"

He looked at the hand on his arm, then gently held it in his. "Etta, calm yourself. There's no sense worrying about these men unless they give us a reason to."

She took a few deep breaths. "Y-you're right. I'm sorry. I don't know what's wrong with me." She fanned herself with her hand and returned to the bench. Mercy! What if they needed their horses tended to? Would she shoe them and get shot for her trouble?

Oliver bent to her. "Stay here." He straightened and left the blacksmith's shop. Captain Stanley was already crossing the street to the saloon. He must have been in the general store. Etta watched him go inside then sighed in relief. Oliver would soon join him and hopefully find out what the strangers wanted. Were they just passing through? Did they plan to stay awhile? Were they looking for someone? Merciful heavens, for all she knew, Agnes' nephew was among them.

"Calm down, you ninny," she scolded aloud. "They're passing through, most likely. There's nothing to worry about.

She left the bench and went out to the street. Dora and Phileas were in front of the hotel, staring at the saloon and the horses tied to the hitching post in front of it. The captain would find out what the strangers were doing here. At least the town had six capable men staying at the hotel. With any luck, there wouldn't be room for the strangers what with all the Darlings rooming there.

She tried not to think about the newcomers, but it was hard. Alma was in front of her store staring at the saloon with the rest of them. Even Mr. Hawthorne was watching from his new hardware store. Good grief, what would the Featherstones do when they finally noticed the strangers?

She didn't get a good look at them, but they weren't

the well-dressed gentlemen the Darlings were. No, these men were rougher looking, unshaven, and she hoped wouldn't stay long.

Dora hurried into the hotel and Etta wondered if it was to tell Mr. McSweeney that they might have more than the usual amount of guests for dinner. Did she dare join Oliver and his brothers tonight? What if the strangers were also there? Would they rob all of them?

"Stop it, Etta." She closed her eyes. Took a few deep breaths and tried to think of something else. If she didn't, she'd work herself up and for what? A handful of strangers who were just passing through?

Etta looked at the saloon again. "So long as they don't go near the bank, we'll be all right." She swallowed hard, and wondered if any of the others staring at the saloon were thinking the same thing.

Chapter Six

Oliver watched the strangers from the table he and Phileas occupied. They'd entered the saloon at almost the same time, both curious as to what the strangers wanted and to the frightful reactions of the townsfolk. Captain Stanley acted indifferently to the newcomers, served them the whiskey they asked for, then asked if they'd like to try his applejack. Two of them did, complimented him, but went back to the whiskey.

Sterling entered the saloon, spied Oliver and Phileas, and headed straight for them. "Well, what have they done so far?" he whispered as he sat.

Phileas leaned his way. "They're just drinking, but they could also be looking for something."

"Yes, like how to rob the town blind," Oliver whispered. He realized he shouldn't have suggested it, especially not after telling Etta not to come to the same conclusion.

"Watch them," Sterling said then left the table for the bar. "Captain, you know what we like."

Captain Stanley gave them a sharp nod and disappeared into the kitchen.

One stranger, the oldest, turned to face them as Sterling returned to the table. "Say that again," he said gruffly.

Sterling glanced at Oliver and Phileas. "I beg your pardon?"

The man laughed. "Did ya hear that boys? He's got himself a fancy accent." He waved his hands back and forth. "Woo-ee!"

Another man laughed. To Oliver he looked like the youngest of the five. "Ya must not be from around here."

"We're not," Phileas said. "Just passing through. You?"

"Yep," said a third, turning to face them. Oliver noticed a resemblance between the three of them— brothers? "What's the name of this town?"

"Apple Blossom," Oliver said. "For all the apples, you see. Not much else is here."

"Trust us, we do see," the oldest one said. "Never would have known this place was here if not for the sign. How far to Virginia City from here?"

"A little over a half day's ride," Sterling said. "Perhaps longer."

The eldest sighed, then reached for his drink. "I ain't riding that far. Let's spend the night."

Oliver looked at his brothers in panic just as Conrad waltzed in. "Afternoon, gentlemen," he greeted. He tipped his hat and headed for their table. "What news?" he asked quietly.

"Passing through," Phileas said, just as low.

Captain Stanley came around the bar with a bottle of apple juice and three glasses. "Deputy, would you like some?"

"Don't mind if I do," Conrad said with a smile.

The eldest of the five turned to face them again. "You talk fancy too." He headed for their table, studying them as he approached. "You fellas kind of look alike."

"That's because we're brothers," Phileas said with a smile. "There's a few in your party that look alike as well."

The man grunted. "They're brothers too." He nodded at the other men at the bar. "That one on the end is their cousin." He eyed Conrad. "Deputy, eh?" He looked at the rest of them. "Passin' through?"

"Yes," Phileas said. "A little visit, then it's back to England."

The man pushed his hat back. "Is that so?" He smiled at Conrad. "Bet you don't get much action in this town."

"You have no idea," Conrad said with an exaggerated roll of his eyes. "Thank goodness my brothers decided to pass through here on their way home or I'd die of boredom."

The man glanced at his cohorts. "That bad, huh?"

"Have you seen this place? I have to make sure the sign is still up on the main road so people know we exist."

"Unfortunately, there's not much here, brother. You should consider a larger community," Sterling said as if disgusted.

Oliver did his best to hide a smile. They were trying to give the strangers reason to leave sooner than later.

"Hotel any good?" the eldest stranger asked.

Conrad smiled. "It's decent. Though I'm not sure how full up it is considering my family is also passing through to visit." He looked at Sterling. "Any rooms left?"

"I don't know. Maybe not."

Conrad smiled at the man again. "Mister...?"

"Name's Frank. I think we'll mosey down to the hotel and find out. I don't fancy campin' out when there are perfectly good beds in town."

"You call this a town?" one of his cohorts laughed.

Oliver and his brothers laughed too. The only one that didn't was Captain Stanley who, though he did smile, retreated behind the bar. He knew what was really going on and would let Oliver and his brothers handle it. No doubt as soon as the lot of them went to the hotel, he'd go to the bank and warn the Featherstones there were strangers in town. That is, if someone hadn't already.

"C'mon, boys, let's go see what the hotel here offers." Frank set his shot glass on the bar, wiped his hand across his mouth, then headed for the swinging doors. His friends did the same and followed. They didn't bother mounting their horses as the hotel was right next door.

"Well, I guess I'll continue my rounds," Conrad said loud enough for the newcomers to hear.

"Do that. We'll head for the hotel and see what's on the menu for dinner," Phileas said. He left the table as the last of the five strangers went out the swinging doors.

"Mind yourselves," Captain Stanley warned, his voice low despite the strangers being gone.

Sterling nodded. "We will." He headed for the doors, Oliver right behind him. Outside on the boardwalk they watched as the man called Frank and the others filed into the hotel.

"I've got to get to Dora." Phileas jogged past. He slowed before he reached the hotel's front windows, then casually walked by them and inside.

"Come along," Sterling said. "Let's see what else we can find out."

"Do you think they'll really spend the night?" Oliver asked.

"One whiff of McSweeney's or Dora's cooking and wild horses couldn't drag them away," Conrad said. "He would pick tonight to make something special."

When they entered the hotel lobby, Dora was behind the counter, handing Frank a pen so he could sign in. They still didn't know if the strangers were friends or foes, and she would not turn away customers who might pass word around that Apple Blossom had a lovely little hotel. The town was seeing the benefit of growing, and more and more folks were seeing what they could do to make that happen.

Frank signed the register. "Glad we got the last two rooms. We thank ya, miss."

She smiled, nodded, then handed them two keys. "I'll bring up some extra blankets. I'm sorry one of you will have to sleep on a cot, but it's all we have with the other folks staying in town."

Frank looked over his shoulder at them. "How many of ya are there?"

Sterling smiled. "Six."

"Five," Conrad corrected. "I can't be counted."

Frank nodded, took the keys from Dora, then headed for the staircase.

Oliver and his brothers watched them climb the stairs as Dora hurried down the back hall, probably to get the extra blankets for whichever one of them had to sleep on the cot. As soon as the newcomers disappeared, Oliver sighed. "Are we overreacting?"

"No, we're being cautious, that's all," Sterling said. "As well we should be. But we're keeping our heads. I'm not sure some of the townspeople will. If these men are outlaws, a trigger-happy resident could get people hurt."

"Right," Conrad said. "We'd best warn people, especially the Featherstones." He smiled. "In fact, we could empty the bank vault."

Sterling grinned. "That's a good idea. Let them think no one in town has any money." He slapped Conrad on the back. "Brilliant."

Oliver smiled. "I'll run to the bank and tell the Featherstones."

Sterling nodded in approval and Oliver was off like a shot.

Etta watched Oliver leave the hotel and followed. She wanted to know what was going on but wasn't about to go into the hotel to find out. So far, the strangers had left their horses at the saloon. Would they bring them to her soon? She should wait and find out, but couldn't stand not knowing if Oliver and his brothers had found out any information about the five men.

She hurried up the street and stopped when Alma hissed. "Etta!"

Etta looked at her, then the hotel. "What?" She glanced at the hotel again. She hoped they had nothing to worry about from the strangers, but that's what everyone assumed the last time a handful came through town.

Alma hurried down the steps from the boardwalk to the street. "Well? Do you know anything about them?"

"No, but I just saw Oliver head up the street." She pointed. "He's heading straight for the bank, I bet."

Alma nodded as Mr. Hawthorne headed their way from his hardware shop. "Ladies," he said and tipped his hat. "Is everything all right? People seem suddenly nervous."

"Of course we're nervous," Alma shot back in a harsh whisper. "There are strangers in town."

Mr. Hawthorne's eyebrows shot up. "I see. And I take it that's bad?"

Alma's face contorted. "Yes!"

He looked sympathetic. "Now I do see. Ladies, it will be handled." He tipped his hat again and headed for the hotel.

"Oh, no. What is he doing?" Alma griped.

"He's probably as curious as the rest of us."

"He does know what happened here, doesn't he?" Alma asked.

"I believe so. But to what extent, I can't say." Etta took a few steps toward the hotel. "I'd better check on Oliver, then get back to the livery stable."

Alma made a shooing motion with one hand and turned to go back inside her store. Etta hoped she didn't lock the doors. What would the strangers think then?

Etta hurried across the street and, lifting her skirt, broke into a run. When she reached the bank she came to a skidding stop and went inside. Oliver was in Mr. Featherstone's office talking with him. Mrs. Featherstone stood next to her husband, her eyes rounded to saucers. "Oh dear." She approached the office slowly so as not to disturb them.

"Mr. Miller!" Mr. Featherstone called as he headed her way.

Etta sidestepped lest she be run over by him.

"Mr. Miller! Open the vault, hurry!"

The bank teller complied without question, looking worried.

Oliver exited the office as Captain Stanley hurried into the bank. "Oliver lad, Conrad just told me the plan." He held up some flour sacks. "I know just where to hide everything!"

"Splendid," Oliver gushed, then noticed her. "Etta, what are you doing here?"

She watched Mr. Miller open the bank's safe, then saw the sacks in Captain Stanley's hands. "What's going on?"

Oliver took her by the shoulders. "We're putting everyone's money in a safe place until after the strangers leave. You can't rob a bank if there's nothing to rob. We'll make sure they know it at dinner tonight."

Her hand flew to her mouth. "You're doing what?"

"I'll explain along the way. They'll want to stable their horses." He took her arm and steered her toward the door. "Come along, I'll help."

"Francis and I will take care of this," the captain called, waving a flour sack at them.

"Jolly good, captain." Oliver saluted him as he ushered Etta out the door.

"You think they'll rob the bank?" she asked. Her breathing picked up and she felt faint. "But, what about Mr. Miller and the Featherstones—what if they get shot?"

"I assure you, they'll be fine. My brothers and I will see to it."

"But..."

"Hush now. Don't speak of it. We don't want anyone to overhear."

She snapped her mouth shut, her belly doing a funny little flip at his gentle tone of voice.

When they reached the livery stable, they went into the blacksmith's shop where Oliver took off his jacket and rolled up his sleeves.

"What are you doing?" she asked.

"Making it look like I'm helping."

"Oh, right." She motioned him to follow her into the stable area. "I've got room in the corral outside for their horses. With the six of you here, all the spare stalls are taken."

"But you can accommodate their tack?"

"Yes, we can put them in the second tack room."

"Excellent." He faced her, putting his hands on her shoulders. They were large, warm and comforting. "Now listen. Act as if nothing is wrong. Show no fear. For all we know they're cowboys returning to their ranch after a cattle drive."

She managed half a smile. "I'll try."

He drew closer. "Try very hard."

She swallowed and nodded.

"Hey, anyone in there?"

She jumped at the sound of the stranger's voice.

Oliver bent to her ear. "Everything's fine. Normal." He looked into her eyes. "And I'm right here."

Part of her melted into a puddle as she nodded again.

"Coming!" Oliver turned her around and they headed for the blacksmith's shop at the other end of the livery stable. "Ah, we meet again," he said to Frank, who must be the leader. "How can we help you?"

Frank glanced between them. "What are ya doin' here?"

"Oh, just helping. Conrad, my brother the deputy? He told me they needed an extra hand down at the livery stable, so here I am."

Frank sneered. "Good Samaritan, eh? Fine, take care of our horses. Mine's the paint. Watch what ya feed him – he's got a delicate stomach."

"Right," Oliver said as he spied the man's horse. "Et ... er, Miss Whitehead, would you mind leading this gentleman's horse to the corral?" He smiled at Frank as she headed for the paint horse. "As I recall, the feed is included in the price, isn't that right, Miss Whitehead?"

She nodded as she took the reins from the man and turned for the corral. She could hear Oliver speaking as she went.

"Where's the owner?" one of the other men asked.

"Um, away."

Etta glanced over her shoulder in time to see Oliver smile at them as he began motioning them toward the corral while reciting the prices for board. They were the same prices she charged the Darlings, and he even offered to groom their horses for them. This pleased the strangers, who tossed Oliver a few extra coins for his trouble. Maybe the five weren't a bunch of murderous outlaws, but time would tell.

She had just reached the corral when she heard the distinct sound of a stagecoach. Oh, dear! Now what? The stage only came to town when there was mail to be delivered, or to bring Alma something she ordered, or, on the rare occasion, a passenger. Could Agnes' nephew be coming?

She led the paint into the corral and loosened the cinch to unsaddle him as the stage entered town and pulled up in front of the general store in a cloud of dust.

"I wonder if that's the doctor," Oliver said.

Frank looked at his cohorts. "Ya mean this town don't even have a doctor?"

"If that's him, it does now," Oliver said. "They've been waiting for one."

The men laughed. "I bet this place don't even have a preacher," one chortled.

"It doesn't," Oliver quickly said. "This place has nothing."

Frank smacked him on the back. "No wonder yer brother told the deputy he should think about goin' somewhere else. Maybe ya should take him back to England."

Oliver nodded as the stagecoach's door opened. "Good idea."

The men continued to laugh as they led their horses into the corral and began to untack them.

Etta breathed a sigh of relief and hefted the saddle and blanket off the paint horse.

"I'll take those, missy," Frank said. He took the tack from her.

"There's an empty tack room inside – you can store your gear there."

"Egad!"

All heads turned as Oliver backed up, smacking into one of the strangers.

"Hey, watch where yer going!"

Oliver turned to him. "T-terribly sorry." He spun on his heel, mouth agape.

Everyone stared at him, then at the middle-aged woman getting off the stage. As soon as she did, she whacked the stagecoach driver with her parasol.

"Oliver," Etta said. "Who is that? Do you know her?"

He nodded as he cringed. "Yes," he squeaked.

Frank and his men looked at him, then the passenger. "Well?" one of them said. "Who is it?" The rest of the men's faces screwed up as they, too, looked at the middle-aged woman in the fancy clothes.

"Don't tell me she's a relative of yers?" Frank asked.

Oliver cringed again and nodded. "Unfortunately, yes."

Etta gaped at him. "Who?"

He looked at her and gulped. "*That* is my mother."

Chapter Seven

"**Y**our mother?!" Etta said, voice cracking.

"Does she talk fancy like you?" one man asked.

"She sure looks like it," Frank commented. He glanced as his friends. "Let's finish with the horses, then find us some grub. I'm hungry." He glanced at Oliver. "The food at the hotel good?"

Oliver, in shock, nodded. His parents hadn't seen him yet. What were they doing here?! And how did they even know where to look? He heard one door opening at the hotel, saw Phileas come out, take one look at their parents, then do an about-face and hurry back inside, slamming the door behind him. Coward. Oliver cleared his throat. "Dear me, why do I have to be the one?"

"To do what?" Etta asked.

He glanced at her. "Face the firing squad. No, one of those would have more mercy." He pulled at his jacket, ran his hand through his hair, then cleared his throat again. Father was speaking to the stagecoach driver. He must have upset Mother. Why else would she clobber him over the head with her parasol?

"Aren't you going to talk to them?" Etta asked.

He stepped behind the livery stable wall, which formed one side of the corral. "I can't understand why they're here. How did they find us?"

Etta shrugged. "Did you ask for money?"

One man unsaddling horses looked their way, then got back to work. Oliver glanced at him and sighed. "Me, no. Even if someone sent a telegraph asking for funds, they'd have gone through our solicitor. We each have our own bank accounts."

"You're not happy to see them, are you?"

"I still can't fathom they're here. Oh, bother."

Frank and his cohorts carried tack from the corral into the livery stable. "I'd better make sure they know where to put everything," Etta remarked, looking Oliver over. "Are you going to be okay? You look pale."

"I have no doubt. Perhaps I'll drown myself in the horse trough. It would be preferable to what awaits me." Good grief, how much more pathetic could he be?

Etta's eyebrows knit in concern. "Oliver, are you sure you're all right?"

He nodded and waved her to the corral's gate. "Fine. See about your business while I deal with this."

"You make it sound as if you're about to be hanged."

He nodded. "I could only hope."

Her face screwed up in confusion as she left the corral and headed into the livery stable. No sooner had he closed the gate, he heard the familiar screech of fury. "Oliver!"

He closed his eyes a moment. "Yes, Mother?" He turned to face his parents, surprise on his face. "What are you doing here?"

"I might ask the same of you!" She opened her parasol and held it over her head. "Oliver Wendell Darlington, what's the meaning of this? And where are your brothers?"

He gulped. Phileas was probably rounding them up – those he could find, that is. "Here and there. How did you find us?"

She narrowed her eyes and pulled a folded piece of paper out of her reticule. "With this!" She stomped over and handed it to him.

"What is it, a telegraph message?" He took it from her and read aloud. "Dear Mr. and Mrs. Darlington, you should know that your sons are in Apple Blossom in Montana Territory and plan to marry without telling you. Considering your station, I thought you ought to know. AGNES FEATHERSTONE!"

"There's no need to yell," Father said as he joined them. "Ollie my boy." He pulled him into his arms and patted him on the back. "Where's Sterling?" He looked around as if Sterling might be hiding behind a bale of hay.

Oliver looked up the street at the bank. Sure enough,

Agnes was standing outside, watching them. Was she ever going to get a talking to!

"Oliver!" Mother snapped. "Where are your brothers?"

He tried not to roll his eyes and nodded toward the hotel. "Follow me." He trudged across the street.

"Oliver!" his father called this time. He stood next to a pile of luggage.

"Yes, of course." Oliver grabbed what he could, then headed for the hotel again.

Phileas stepped outside with a forced smile. "Mother, Father, whatever are you doing here?"

Oliver scowled at him as he brushed past into the lobby. "Dora?"

Dora hurried down the hall from the kitchen and took up her post behind the counter. "Phileas just told me. Merciful heavens, do I look all right?" She patted her hair and tried to look past him. "They're coming in?"

Oliver let the luggage drop with a thud. "I'm afraid so."

Her hand flew to her mouth. "How did they find you?" she whispered.

He frowned as he handed her the telegraph message.

Dora quickly perused it. "Agnes!"

He slowly nodded. "I'd like to know how she got the information to do this."

"So would Phileas and the others. When was Agnes ever around to glean anything?"

"I have no idea, but I intend to find out." He turned

to the doors, in no hurry to help Phileas with their parents. Let him deal with them for a moment.

Jean hurried from the kitchen. "Oliver," she said, skidding to a stop and looking out the windows of the double doors. "Oh, dear. Wallis went to find Sterling. He looked terrified."

"As well he should," Oliver grumbled.

"What are they doing here?" Dora held up the telegraph message, and Jean read it and gasped. "No!"

"Yes," Dora said. "The question is, how?"

Jean's face twisted up. "Agnes must have overheard something, maybe pieces of conversation, and put it all together."

"We were so careful. Everyone was," Oliver said. "Everything about who we really are was spoken alone, in private."

Jean paled as Wallis came down the hall with Sterling in tow. "I just had a thought." She spun to Wallis. "They're here because of Agnes."

"What?!" Sterling and Wallis said at once.

Jean held up the telegraph message. Sterling snatched it from her and read it. "Oh, bloody..."

"Language." Wallis took it and read. "Oh bleeding..." His eyes flicked around the room. "... bother." He looked at Jean. "I... think this is my fault."

"Doesn't matter whose fault it is," Sterling said. "We'll deal with it." He took a deep breath. "Hold your ground. They are *not* talking us into returning to

England until we're good and ready. We stick to our plan."

"Right," Wallis agreed.

Oliver was silent. So far, there wasn't much of a plan for him other than to go home and act as moral support for Phileas and Dora. He sighed. "Let's get this over with."

Sterling grabbed his arm. "You shouldn't have to be the one to explain things." He glanced at the door. "If I know Phileas, he's pouring on the charm, not that it will do us any good." He sighed, then headed outside. Oliver and Wallis followed while Jean and Dora remained inside. They didn't need to get trapped in the heat of battle.

"Well, there you are," Mother said as they closed the door behind them. "About time you showed up." She went to Sterling and pointed at her cheek.

He kissed it. "Mother." He shook Father's hand. "Sir, it's good to see you."

"Hmmm, of course it is," Father mumbled. "Sounds like we got here in the nick of time."

Sterling glanced at Oliver and Wallis, then Phileas. "Dare I ask?"

Father smiled. "Why, in time to attend some weddings, from the sound of it."

"We'll do nothing of the kind!" Mother squawked. "How dare you say you're in love! And that goes for all of you!" Her eyes settled on Oliver. "Except you, dear. At least you've got some sense!"

Oliver sighed. "Mother, let Sterling explain."

"I don't want to hear excuses," she spat, then spun to Sterling. "Pack your things. We're leaving on the next stage out of here."

Sterling shook his head. "Mother, as hard as this is for you to believe, I'm in love. So is Irving, Conrad, Phileas, and Wallis. We all fell in love with kind, generous, God-fearing women who love us in return."

Oliver fought the urge to take a step back. His mother's pinched expression made Agnes Featherstone's look downright sweet in comparison. "You will break off any engagements you have, is that clear?"

"Now, Cordelia," Father said. "Let's not get angry."

She spun to him. "I am not angry, I am seething!"

Oliver pinched the bridge of his nose. Reasoning with Mother would be harder than any of them thought. This squabble could easily turn into an outright war.

Etta watched Oliver and his parents and brothers from the safety of the blacksmith's shop. The men who rode into town had stowed their tack and were heading across the street. Considering the number of people in town, she doubted Dora had any rooms left. Where would Mrs. Darling ... wait a minute. When Oliver read the telegram, (yes, she'd been eavesdropping) the name wasn't Darling, but Darlington. "Why would Agnes write to a Mr. and Mrs. Darlington?" She scratched her head in confusion, then her armpit.

"Howdy."

She jumped. "Goodness gracious!"

"Name's Jonny. I didn't mean to scare ya."

She turned to the man. Of the five, he looked to be the youngest. He was still, however, just as unshaven, dirty, and ill-kept as the rest. "Oh, hello. Aren't you going to the hotel to get something to eat?"

He took off his hat as he looked her up and down. "In a spell. I thought I'd talk to ya first." He licked his lips.

Etta backed up a step. "What do you want? Does your horse need shoeing?"

"Nah, he's fine." His eyes raked over her again. "So are you. What's your name?"

"Miss Whitehead. My father and I own this blacksmith shop and livery stable."

He nodded as his eyes skipped over everything. "Your pa, huh? Where's he at?"

She swallowed. "Um, up the road." She wasn't going to mention he was *buried* up the road. The less the man knew, the better.

Jonny nodded as his stomach growled. "Guess I am hungry." He looked at the hotel. "What do you know about them fancy folks?"

"About as much as you do."

"Hmmm." Without another word, he headed across the street.

Etta's shoulders slumped as she let out the breath she was holding. She didn't like the hungry look in Jonny's eye. Pa told her to stay away from men with that sort of look and she planned to.

She watched the men file past Oliver and his family and go inside the hotel. Phileas watched them, nodded to Sterling, and the two men went inside leaving their parents with Oliver and Wallis. She had no idea where Irving and Conrad were. The former might be at Sarah's house with his future family while the latter was probably doing rounds with Sheriff Cassie. What would their parents do when they found out one of their sons was the town deputy?

She shoved the thought aside and wondered if she should still take Oliver up on his invitation to have dinner with him and his brothers. It wouldn't be the best idea, judging from the high pitch of his mother's voice and how it carried across the street and into the shop. Even the strangers gave Mrs. Darling (Darlington?) a wide berth as they entered the hotel. Dora would probably serve them sandwiches then head across the street to Alma's for more supplies if she didn't have enough to feed everyone tonight.

Curious, Etta wandered down the street to the general store and joined Alma on the bench outside. "Hello."

Alma didn't take her eyes off the scene in front of the hotel. "Afternoon, Etta. That's their mother."

"And their father."

"Here in Apple Blossom."

"Yes."

She looked at Etta. "Doesn't that seem strange?" She leaned forward and looked past Etta to see up the street. "I see Agnes finally went back inside the bank."

Etta looked too. "Mm-hmm. Captain Stanley and Mr. Featherstone are hiding the money in case the strangers turn out to be bank robbers."

Alma's eyes widened. "What?"

Etta covered her mouth with her hands, realizing her mistake. "Tell no one, Alma. Understand?" She lowered her voice. "If those men turn out to be bad, they can't know the townspeople have money. Once they find out there isn't any in the bank, maybe they'll leave."

Alma glanced at the hotel. "I think they'll leave anyway. Who wants to stay in a hotel with that?"

Another screech echoed across the street. It sounded like "Conrad" followed by "lawman," but Etta couldn't be sure. All she knew was that Oliver's mother was giving him and poor Wallis what for. She hoped Sterling or Phileas returned soon to rescue them. She folded her hands in her lap and sighed. "I wonder how long they'll stay?"

"I wonder what Letty, Sarah and Cassie will do when they come to town."

Etta nodded. "I hope Conrad and Irving are with them when they do."

"Me too."

They sat in silence a few moments as Oliver's mother continued her tirade. They were stuck between a hotel full of potential outlaws, and the Darlings' parents.

Surely their mother would tire soon and go inside. But then what? If Dora had to turn her away because they were full up...

Dora suddenly appeared, skirted around Oliver and the others, and hurried across the street. "Alma!"

Alma got to her feet. "What do you need?"

"Can I stay with you tonight?"

"What?"

Etta stood. "Why?"

Dora glanced over her shoulder. "Because I'm giving my rooms to Phileas' parents. There's no place else for them to stay."

"Oh, Dora, no," Etta sighed.

"What else can I do?"

Alma nodded at the hotel. "Looks like they're going inside."

"I told Jean to check them in. Good thing I put fresh sheets on my bed this morning."

Alma gave her a sympathetic pat on the arm. "Come inside and tell me what you need."

Dora followed her, as did Etta. She didn't know what she could do to help other than offer a listening ear.

Dora took a deep breath, then rattled off a list. "I'll need another ten pounds of flour, five pounds of sugar, four pounds of coffee, and let's see, better give me some carrots, a few onions and..." She headed for the displays of fruits and vegetables.

"Do you need any help cooking?" Etta called after her. She was a terrible cook, but offered all the same.

"No, I have Jean and Sarah to help me." She gathered some potatoes. "I think."

"Is Sarah coming back into town?" Alma asked.

"Good question," Etta said. Sarah and her children had moved back into their house for the time being. As soon as she and Irving were wed, Jean and Wallis would buy Sarah's house and move in while Sarah and Irving took up residence in the building Irving had purchased.

Etta leaned against the counter as Alma helped Dora gather what she needed. How long ago did Agnes send that telegraph message? It had to have been weeks. It would take at least that long for Oliver's parents to get to America and take a train west. She knew Oliver and his brothers had sent word to their parents that they were staying longer in America, and all had made mention that it might not go over well. But which message did they get first? Their sons' or Agnes'?

Either way, their parents didn't like the idea of their sons marrying Americans and wanted them all to come home. She didn't see that happening. Oliver's brothers loved their future wives and had come up with a plan that would hopefully satisfy all. Now all they had to do was convince their parents of that.

Chapter Eight

Finally, Mother and Father moved into the lobby. There was no sign of the strangers that rode into town, and Oliver concluded they'd wolfed down some sandwiches and retreated to their rooms. He saw Dora hurry across the street a few moments ago and wondered if she went for more supplies. The hotel was full, and there were no rooms left. He supposed he could bunk with Wallis or Irving ...

"Good afternoon," Jean said with a friendly smile. "Welcome to the Apple Blossom Hotel. May I help you?"

"You may," Mother huffed. "We want your finest room."

Jean smiled again, but this time it was forced. Her next words looked like they pained her and Oliver cringed. "We have a lot of guests staying at the hotel at the moment, but we have... a suite of rooms available."

"Good," Mother said. "We'll take them." She looked

down her nose at Jean. "I require a bath. Does this hotel have hot running water?"

Jean went pink. "I'm afraid not."

"Mother, it's fine," Oliver said. "We can haul water to your room."

"What?!" she snapped. "You'll do nothing of the kind." She turned back to Jean. "Young woman, I'll need two maids."

Jean glanced at Oliver and back. "We don't have maids."

Mother's eyes bulged. "What? No maids?!"

"Now, dearest, this isn't England," Father said. "You must remember, this is still unsettled territory, full of outlaws and brigands. We're lucky they have accommodations of this caliber." He looked around and nodded in satisfaction. "This is a quaint place, don't you agree?"

Jean nodded, as did Oliver, as they waited for his mother to say something.

She took in the new wallpaper and other improvements Phileas and Dora had made. "I suppose it's not as bad as it could be." She gave her attention back to Jean. "Key."

Jean closed her eyes a moment, then reached into her apron pocket and pulled out a key. "I should let you know that in order to accommodate your stay, the owner of the hotel has given up her rooms for you."

Mother and Father exchanged a look of surprise. "Well," Mother said. "It's nice to know that some people around here have manners." She snatched the key from Jean and looked toward the staircase.

"The rooms are just down this hall." Jean came out from behind the counter. "Follow me."

"Oliver, Wallis," Mother called over her shoulder. "We shan't be long. Don't go anywhere."

Father sighed. "Will one of you boys help me with the luggage?"

"Of course, Father." Oliver picked up the heavier pieces and headed for Dora's rooms. Wallis followed with what was left.

When they entered Dora's parlor Mother said nothing. Instead, she went to the window and stared out. "If not for the circumstances, I suppose this place might be charming." She spun on her heel to face them. "On second thought, I'm tired. Your father and I will speak to you at dinner. Don't be late."

"When have any of our sons been late to a meal?" Father laughed.

She arched an eyebrow at him, and he cleared his throat and reached for a valise.

Oliver backed toward the door. "We'll be going now."

Mother gave them a curt nod but said nothing as she examined the door to the bedroom.

Oliver backed out of the room, Wallis following. As soon as they were in the hall, they shut the door and sighed in relief. "Great Scott," Wallis whispered. "What are we going to do?"

"Exactly what Sterling said. Hold our ground." He put his hand on his brother's shoulder. "Remain steadfast, Wallis."

"Easy for you to say, you're unattached. I'm going to have to fight for my future bride to make sure she stays one. Who knows what Mother will threaten us with just to get her way."

Oliver gulped. He didn't want to think about it. He also didn't want to wind up a sacrificial lamb. As the only remaining son with no betrothed, Mother was bound to throw all her energy at him. Whatever peace he had would be gone. As would his brothers—they'd hightail it to Virginia City to wed as fast as they could now. But first they'd try to talk Mother and Father into giving their blessing. If they could get that, they could avoid verbal bloodshed. Mother was most proficient at inflicting it and wouldn't hesitate to do so.

"I'd better check on Jean," he heard Wallis say.

Oliver nodded but said nothing. He was hungry and should eat something. Hmm, was there anything left *to* eat? With the commotion of their parents' arrival, the newcomers might have devoured everything Dora prepared for lunch.

When he entered the kitchen, Dora looked at him with a relieved smile. "Oh, thank goodness it's you. Did your mother and father get settled in?"

"They're probably unpacking as we speak." He glanced at the kitchen door leading to the hall. "Then again, perhaps not."

"What do you mean?"

He went to the stove. Nothing was cooking. "No lunch?"

Dora held up a finger then went to the icebox and pulled out a plate of sandwiches. "Here, take one."

"Thank you." He stared at it a moment. "You believe Phileas will do all he can to convince our mother that he's in love with you."

"Of course, but even if she believes it, will that keep her from threatening to disinherit him?"

Oliver went to the table and sat as Dora brought him a plate. "It's hard to say. She wanted all of us to marry women of high social rank. With large dowries, of course." He took a bite of sandwich and enjoyed the taste of ham, lettuce and mustard. He didn't like a lot of mayonnaise and Dora knew it. This sandwich she'd made especially for him. In fact, she knew all their individual likes and dislikes, more than their own mother and cook did. He was going to miss Dora's attention to detail with her cooking and baking.

"Oliver, are you all right? You're quite pale."

He touched his cheek. "Am I?"

She nodded and brought him a napkin.

"Thank you." He took it and dabbed at his mouth before taking another bite. Maybe by the time he was done with his sandwich, he would have woken up from this nightmare and things would be back to normal. Now that his parents had shown up, he realized how much he liked Apple Blossom. It was a respite from the life he had in England, and he understood why his brothers all loved it so. They didn't just want to make sure their betrotheds could still live here, they wanted to as well.

He finished his sandwich in silence and wondered where Sterling had gotten to. He imagined he was looking for Irving and Conrad to give them the news. Hmmm, maybe Conrad could arrest Mother and lock her up for a few days, then send her off on a stagecoach for the journey home. He smiled at the thought. Too bad it would never happen.

"Frank Jones," Dora said.

"I beg your pardon?"

She crossed her arms in front of her. "Frank Jones, Herb Green, Jonny Green, Dale Green, and last but not least, Dilbert Green."

He cocked his head. "The strangers?"

"Yes. Do you think those are their real names?"

"I'm afraid I don't have the foggiest." He pushed the empty plate away and sat back in his chair. "What's for dinner?"

She laughed. "Always thinking with your stomach. Mr. McSweeney was going to cook, but we decided with all the extra mouths to feed that fried chicken was in order. I just hope I have enough."

"Oh dear, I invited Etta. I shouldn't have done that."

"You did?" She bit her lip. "It's all right. But you'd better remind her. My guess is with all the hotel guests, she won't come unless you do."

"She's that forgetful?"

"No, she's that... how should I say this? Courteous? She won't want to take food from someone, especially if they're a hotel guest."

He smiled. "Then I'd better go speak with her." He left the table and headed for the door leading to the dining room. "Green, eh?"

"That's what they wrote in the register."

"Those are not the same names of the men that stayed here before?"

She looked at the floor. "No."

He tried to make his smile reassuring. "Good." He left the hotel and went down the street to the blacksmith's shop. Mother had upset things, but the strangers were still a concern. "Etta?"

She popped up from the other side of the forge; her left cheek smeared with soot. "Oliver, what are you doing here?"

"I came to remind you of dinner." He pulled his handkerchief from his pants pocket and went to her. "It should prove to be a very interesting evening."

"Made more interesting if Agnes was there. I saw Sterling head up the street a while ago."

"He wouldn't speak to her as yet. He's more interested in finding Irving and Conrad."

She took a poker and stirred the embers of the forge. "How are your parents?"

He leaned against a workbench. "Cranky. But that's not saying much. Mother is always in a foul mood when she's not getting what she wants. In this case, she's not getting a lot."

Etta cringed. "She scares me."

He laughed. "Me too."

She smiled, then looked at the handkerchief in his hand. "What's that for?"

"Oh, allow me." He wiped away the soot on her cheek. "You will still come to dinner?"

"Are you sure there's room?"

He did a quick count in his head. "If there isn't, then some of us can eat out back on blankets. It will be fun. Mr. McSweeney and Dora won't mind." His eyes widened. "Poor Mr. McSweeney. Wait until he meets our mother."

Etta cringed again. "I thought he was making some special dinner."

"He was, but with recent events, Dora has reverted to fried chicken with the usual fare. McSweeney didn't plan on so many people."

"No one did."

Oliver nodded, noting the hint of fear in Etta's eyes. Best he try to take care of that right now.

Etta couldn't get over everything that had happened so far that day. A passel of rough strangers rode into town, then the Darlings' parents arrived. What next?

Etta looked nervously at Oliver. She didn't like

change, and this was upsetting her routine. She didn't have time to fish for her dinner either, so she'd have to take Oliver up on his invitation or eat apples for her evening meal. Again.

"Is everything all right?" he asked gently.

"Yes, of course." She watched him put the soiled handkerchief back in his pocket. "That's going to stain. I'm sorry."

"Don't be. I'm sure Dora can get the stain out." He glanced around the shop. "Perhaps it's best you don't mention your house to my parents just yet. Mother is still upset and will be for a day or two. But once she hears everything we have to say about Apple Blossom and what we've done here, she'll come around."

Etta smiled. "You don't sound convinced."

He stuck his hands in his pockets. "I'm not. I'm trying to convince myself."

She giggled. My, she hadn't giggled in a long time. "You'd better keep trying."

Oliver smiled. "I suppose things could be worse. They could have shown up right after I got sprayed by that skunk."

She laughed.

"Come to think of it," he continued, "if the strangers and my parents had all shown up then, they'd have left posthaste."

Etta laughed harder. "And miss the dance?"

He looked into her eyes, and her belly did a little flip. "Yes, not even a dance could have made them stay. My parents are unaccustomed to skunks and would have found the smell beyond foul." He rocked toe to heel a few times. "You wouldn't care to help me find some skunks, would you?"

She giggled again. "No." She began to tidy up the shop and call it a day. "Aren't you the least bit happy to see them?"

"Well... it's nice that they came. I've often wondered what they'd think of this place. I've even imagined them coming here to visit their grandchildren."

She smiled as her chest warmed. "How nice."

"Unfortunately, these circumstances are different, and I imagine Sterling and the rest of my brothers will have a chat with Mr. Featherstone before long. Agnes had no business sending a telegraph message to our parents."

"She had to have done it weeks ago."

"Wallis and Jean think she overheard them talking after he proposed. He told me they ran into her beyond the torch light of the dance area. She was heading back to the dance and he figured he could speak freely to Jean. That's when Agnes probably heard where we're from."

She noted he said nothing about their name and pondered asking him, but now was not the time. There was too much else going on. "What time is dinner?"

He pulled out his pocket watch and flipped it open. "Six o'clock."

"I'll be there."

"I can escort you."

She laughed again. "That's hardly necessary."

"On the contrary, if my mother is going to have a conniption, I might as well add to it."

She smiled as her heart sank a little. Oliver wasn't falling in love with anyone in Apple Blossom, especially not now. "What will your parents do if your brothers refuse to return to England with them?"

"We have no idea. But one thing we can count on, Mother spews threats when she's not getting what she wants."

She picked up a bucket of water and headed out back with it.

"Here, let me take that." He took the bucket and carried it for her. "You must understand, my mother is the type to have our lives all planned. We're not fitting into those plans at the moment, which is why she's upset."

"But I don't understand. Your brothers are in love. Letty, she's my friend." She sighed. "My only friend when I think about it. I've never seen her so happy. She's just as in love with Sterling as he is with her. Why does your mother insist you all marry English women?"

He shrugged. "Because that's how things have been done for eons where I come from. The thought of her sons marrying uncouth Americans is more than the old girl can take. Sad but true."

Etta nodded but couldn't help feeling like he wasn't telling her everything. "Well, I'll see you at six."

"Can I help you?" He looked around. "Um, shall I dump this anywhere?"

"You can dump it in my bathroom. You are going to put one in, aren't you?"

He smiled. "We are. Phileas drew one into the plans. I'm not sure how good we'll be at putting in the plumbing, but the captain said he can help with that."

"He's a man of many talents." She headed for the area where Oliver and his brothers planned to build her little house. "Speaking of which, have you seen the captain or Mr. Featherstone?"

"They're supposed to..." He glanced around, probably making sure they were alone. "They went to hide the bank's money, remember?"

"Yes, but they've been gone for hours."

He smiled. "Perhaps the captain is drawing Mr. Featherstone a map so he can find the money again."

She smiled. "Perhaps." She followed him until he stopped. "What are you doing?"

"Do you have your key?"

"What?"

"To the front door?"

Etta laughed. "Let me see, I must have it somewhere." She patted the pockets of her leather apron. "Here it is." She handed him the imaginary key.

He inserted it into the equally imaginary lock. "After you," he said and motioned her inside.

Etta stepped into her make-believe parlor and looked

around. "Will Phileas wallpaper my place like he did the others?"

"You have to ask?" Oliver shook his head. "Tsk-tsk-tsk." He went to the back of the house and into the kitchen. "We added a small room off the back porch." He pointed to the far left wall. "That will be the bathroom." He headed that way, opened an imaginary door, then pretended to step in. "Down it goes."

She watched him, giddy inside, as he emptied the bucket into her future commode. If only his parents hadn't showed up along with the strangers, she'd be enjoying this a lot more.

Chapter Nine

Herbert paced back and forth. "I don't know about this town. There ain't nothing here."

Frank lay on the bed, his fingers laced over his chest. "They do have a bank. I suppose we could rob it. Has anyone seen a sheriff?"

"Maybe they don't have one," Jonny said. "The little lady at the blacksmith shop is pretty enough to take along with us."

Frank rolled his eyes. "That's probably the dumbest idea I've ever heard."

Dilbert, who was practicing his quick draw on the other side of the room, glanced at Jonny. "I think she was right pretty."

"Don't matter what ya think," Frank said. "Abductin' someone is a bad idea. Besides, if she's the daughter of a blacksmith, we wouldn't get much ransom for her."

Jonny grinned. "Who said anything about ransom?" He smiled at Dilbert and started laughing. Dilbert holstered his gun and did the same.

"Shut up, both of you," Herbert said. "Can't you see Frank is trying to think?"

Dale, who sat in a chair against the wall, shrugged. "I thought we were just here to spend the night. These folks have nothing worth taking."

"They still have a bank," Frank repeated.

"Yeah," Herbert said. "But who knows if there's any money in it." He moved the lace curtains aside and peeked out the window. "Do we have enough supplies?"

Dilbert joined him at the window. "They got a nice looking little general store."

"I still say this town has..." Dale never got to finish, as a high-pitched screech reached their ears.

Frank sat up. "Jumpin' Jehoshaphat, what was that?"

Dale looked at his legs, spread them, and tried to peek under his chair. He looked at the others, then lowered his voice. "I think it came from downstairs." He pointed at the grate in the floor.

Jonny giggled. "I bet it's that uppity English couple that showed up. Boy, have they caused a stir!"

Frank left the bed, went to Jonny and smacked him on the back. "Will ya shut up?"

"... And another thing, Charles!" came the voice from the grate. "I'll disinherit those boys before I see them wed a bunch of country bumpkins from America!"

"Dearest!"

Jonny giggled again. So did Dale, who moved the chair, got down on his hands and knees and put his ear to the grate.

Frank rolled his eyes and went to the window. "We better get a few more supplies while we're here."

"They'll not see a penny of our fortune if they wed those women!"

Frank slowly turned toward the others, who were now gathered around the grate to listen. "What was that?" he whispered.

Herbert motioned him over. "I think they have money."

Frank joined them, his ear turned toward the floor. "How much?"

"But dearest, can't you see reason?" came the man's voice. "Sterling will be the next Viscount Darlington and see to the running of the estate. So what if he marries an American?"

"She'll not get a cent!" his wife screeched back.

Frank's eyes lit up. "They do have money!" He rubbed his hands together in glee. "Gather 'round boys," he whispered, quickly motioning them to the other side of the room. "I think we *will* take someone with us when we leave."

"The blacksmith's daughter?" Jonny said hopefully.

"No, you idiot—that harpy down there. If that English fella has plenty of money, and I'm thinking he does, considerin' he owns an estate, then the old crow's gotta be worth somethin'."

Herbert scratched his head. "She didn't look that old to me."

Frank rolled his eyes again and counted to ten. These were four of the dumbest outlaws he'd ever worked with. He wasn't sure they were going to make it. "We abduct the woman, hold her for ransom, and while we have her, mosey over to Virginia City and rob the bank there. That'll give that English fella time to get some money together so he can get his wife back."

"Sounds good to me," Herbert said. "What do you think, boys?"

His brothers and cousin nodded their heads.

"Then it's settled," Frank said. "Now all we hafta do is figure out when to grab her."

"But why stop there?" Jonny said. "Why not take the blacksmith's daughter...?"

"Will you stop bringing her up?" Herbert snapped.

Dale picked at his teeth with his pinky finger. "If you're going to take anyone, I'd take the banker's wife. At least then he'd use whatever money was in the bank to get her back."

Everyone stared at him a moment.

Dale shrugged. "What?"

"I hate to admit this," Frank said, "but that's a right fine idea."

"The blacksmith's daughter?" Jonny said.

"No!" his brothers barked.

"Keep your voices down." Frank glanced at the floor grate. "One of ya go down to the bank and check things out. I wanna know what the banker's wife looks like."

"But Frank," Jonny whispered. "What if he ain't got a wife?"

"Then we'll just take the Englishwoman. Simple." Frank smacked Jonny upside the head.

"Yeah," Herbert said. "Simple." He smacked Jonny on the other side of his head.

"Ow," Jonny cried. "What did you do that for, Herb?"

"Because you're an idiot. Now you and Dale get down to the bank and see what's what. And while you're at it, see if there's any money."

Frank pinched the bridge of his nose. "Of course, there's money, you imbecile. It's a bank."

"Then why don't we rob it?" Dilbert asked.

Frank pulled at his hair. "Because it's not worth the trouble. Besides, we'll still get the bank's money. I'm sure the banker will use it to pay the ransom. This way we don't have to leave here guns a-blazing and have one of these yahoos ride to Virginia City and warn everyone about us. If we take their women, they'll keep their mouths shut."

The Coolidge brothers and cousin exchanged a look of surprise. "Now why didn't we think of that?" Herbert said.

"I can only imagine," Frank muttered. "Now git."

Jonny and Dale grabbed their hats and went out the door.

"Herbert?" Dilbert said.

"Yeah?"

"What's a vye count?"

"I have no idea. Someone that counts?"

Frank's fingers twitched as he reached for his gun. If he shot them now, he'd have half the headache. "It's some kind of title. One of those English things."

"Title of what?" Dilbert asked. "A book?"

Frank made a face. A solo career was looking better and better. If he shot all four of them, he could add "murderer" to his reputation of being a fast-drawing, tough outlaw.

"Maybe it's a title of a song," Herbert suggested.

Frank cringed. That did it. After they robbed the bank in Virginia City and collected the ransom for the women, he'd take the loot and scoot. The Coolidges were on their own after that.

"I sure hope the banker's got a wife," Herbert said as he sat on the bed. "Then that's twice the money."

"Yeah, considering there's five of us, there's more to split up." Dilbert put on his hat. "I'm gonna mosey across the street to the store. I want some candy."

Frank's eyes narrowed. "Don't get any ideas about abducting the storekeeper, got it?"

Dilbert gave him an innocent look. "What? Me? She probably ain't worth nothing."

"I don't know," Herbert mused. "The owners of a general store in a place like this usually have the most money next to the banker."

Frank facepalmed. "Enough! We have our plan, now let's stick to it. If you want to go to the general store and get a few supplies, then do it now."

Herbert and Dilbert exchanged a look and headed for the door. They tried to go through it together, failed, then scrambled out one at a time, slamming it behind them.

Frank shook his head, sat in the nearest chair and sighed. "Either we're gonna get away with this or the four of them'll be the death of me. Idjits."

Oliver came down the hotel stairs just in time to see two of the strangers leave. He crossed the lobby into the dining room and entered the kitchen where Jean and Dora were both busy cooking. "Etta will join us," he announced. "I'll fetch her when it's time and escort her to dinner." He gave them a boyish grin.

Jean smiled and shook her head as she stirred a pot. "Really, Oliver, take a second look at Etta."

"Second look?" he said in surprise.

Dora nodded. "She's really quite fetching when she's not covered in dirt and ashes."

Oliver crossed to the table. "I'm sure she is. However, the fact remains that I am leaving. And after my parents' visit, may never be allowed to return." He stared at the floor and sighed.

The women giggled. "We were just suggesting it,"

Jean assured. "Although Etta could do with a nice man. Poor thing." She got back to stirring the pot, then covered it with a lid. "Everyone deserves to have somebody."

He half-smiled. Were they trying to play matchmaker?

Dora began dropping dough into a pan. "Dinner will be ready in less than an hour."

He sat back in his chair and sighed again. "Seems hours have passed since the world turned upside down."

Dora and Jean exchange an anxious look. They knew what he was talking about. "If you are referring to your mother," Dora began. "Then yes, it has been hours."

He straightened. "By Jove, you're right. I'd best go fetch Etta."

Jean smiled. "Dora said you have almost an hour until dinner."

"Well, maybe she needs help with something." He headed for the door. "Cheerio!"

He chuckled as he crossed the dining room to the lobby. Let them think what they wanted. He didn't want to be in the hotel any longer than he had to. He might run into Mother, and he didn't want to have to deal with her right now. Thank heavens she was preoccupied with his brothers, or she'd sink her claws into him and start talking about a certain earl's daughter.

He went out the hotel doors and went down the street to the blacksmith's shop. "Etta?" he called when he entered. No answer. "Etta?" His hands went to his hips.

"Where could she have got to?" He left the shop, went around back, and found Etta standing in the middle of the clearing. No, make that her future parlor. He smiled. "Where will you put it?"

She spun around to face him. "What?"

"Do you play?" He trotted toward her.

"Play what?" She shaded her eyes with her hand against the afternoon sun and smiled at him.

Oliver's chest warmed and he wondered if there was something to what Jean and Dora said earlier. When he reached Etta he noticed she'd washed her face and combed her hair before re-braiding it.

She looked around. "I don't know what you're talking about, Oliver."

"The piano. Do you play?"

"No. But Sarah Crawford does. And the captain, of course. But you already knew that."

"And my mother. Though she still uses a pianoforte. It's a bit of a different instrument. Not like modern pianos."

"Sounds like you're living in the past." She took long strides as if measuring and entered what would be her future kitchen. "I shall put the dining table here."

"Kitchen table," he corrected.

"I don't know, I thought perhaps with the kitchen being so large, I could use it for dining and the other room for something else."

"Nonsense, you must have both in case you entertain. There's nothing quite like a formal dining room for guests."

She arched an eyebrow at him. "Do you have a formal dining room at home?"

"Of course." He tried not to look her over but couldn't help it. She'd put on a clean dress and, even though it was worn, she looked lovely in it. "Dinner is in less than an hour."

She cocked her head. "Then what are you doing here?" She began taking long strides to the other end of her future kitchen. "I want my sink here, and my stove over there, and I shall have an icebox."

Oliver smiled—he could hear the giddiness in her voice. "And where will you put it?"

She pointed at what would be the opposite wall. "There. And if the door to the bathroom is next to the stove, then I won't have far to walk when I haul water for my bath."

"But what if we were to put in the proper plumbing? Phileas wants to do it for the hotel."

Her eyes widened. "Hot water? But how can he afford such a thing? How can any of you, for that matter? I don't expect such a luxury."

He shrugged. "One never knows how your little house will turn out." He stuck his hands in his pockets and kicked at the grass. "Seems our other guests at the hotel have split up. Two of them left just before I came over here. I think they went to the general store. I have no idea where the others are."

"And your parents?"

He tried not to roll his eyes. "I could hear Mother and Father arguing from the second story. They seemed to have calmed down, so I thought I'd take a little walk across the street."

Her eyebrows rose. "Oh, so that's what you're doing. I thought it might be too early to come escort me to dinner."

"Yes, but it's fun to look around your house and picture where things could go. Your parlor will be big enough for a piano if you want one."

She blushed. "I don't play, remember?"

He laughed nervously. Now that he decided he found her attractive, he was suddenly antsy. "Oh, yes. Forgive me."

She smiled sympathetically. "Your mother really has you upset, doesn't she?"

He sighed. "My mother can be a tiresome woman when she wants to be. But I know she has our best interests in mind. Well, not entirely, but it's in there." He looked sheepish. "Somewhere."

"Surely she can't be that bad." Etta approached and stopped a few feet away. "Is she?"

"Like I said, when she wants to be. I told the captain that even the village magistrate is intimidated by her."

"Oh, dear. I suppose she is difficult, then." She picked at a loose thread on her dress and stared at the ground. Was she nervous too?

Oliver was struck with a sudden thought. Did she

find him attractive? If she did, how would he know? Oh, bother. Now he'd have to ask one of his brothers.

She took another step closer. "Thank you, Oliver. For inviting me to dinner." As if on cue, her stomach growled.

He tried not to laugh and smiled instead. "Perhaps a small snack first?"

She bit her lip and blushed. "No, I don't want to impose..."

"Not at all. Allow me to get you something." He offered her his arm.

She stared at it a moment, obviously unsure whether she should take it, then finally looped her arm around his. "Dora won't mind?"

He patted her hand. "Why would she? I say, but she's been feeding the lot of us for how long?"

"Yes, but you're paying her."

"True, but if it makes you feel any better, I'll take care of any cost incurred by your empty belly."

Etta laughed, a bright happy sound that made Oliver's chest swell. Yes, perhaps there was something to what Jean and Dora said after all.

Chapter Ten

Etta's heart fluttered as Oliver escorted her across the street on his arm. Part of her wanted the whole town to see them, but that wasn't going to happen. Most people were home after their day's labors, seeing to chores and preparing their evening meals.

She stopped as they reached the hotel and thought of his parents. Did she really want *them* to see her on Oliver's arm? She didn't want to suffer the same scathing looks Mrs. Darling gave Jean and Dora, nor her cutting remarks. Which reminded her... "Oliver, what is your surname?"

He stopped at the hotel doors. "Oh, that." He heaved a sigh. "I'm afraid I'll have to explain that later. After my brothers and I have spoken with our parents again. But in short, we took the name Darling while in America for protection."

She shook her head. "I don't understand."

He looked into her eyes and a small part of her heart melted. He was concerned about her, or perhaps about the change of name. Was there a problem using their proper surname? Did they have enemies in America? What a terrifying thought.

"Etta," he breathed. "You needn't worry. It was merely a precaution, nothing more."

She nodded, unsure of what to say. She didn't want to pry and especially didn't want to bring the wrath of his mother upon herself. What a nightmare that would be! It was bad enough listening to the woman while sitting outside the general store with Alma.

He led her down the hall and entered the kitchen. "Jean, Dora, I'm raiding the cookie jar."

"What?" Dora said and waved a spoon at him. "Don't you dare eat all of them, Oliver!"

He smiled at Etta and headed for the larder.

She followed him in. "Cookies?"

"It's the only thing around here in abundance at any given time of day." He took a cookie jar off a top shelf and pried off the lid. "Help yourself."

She peered into the jar and pulled two sugar cookies out. "Thank you."

He took two for himself, crammed on the lid and put it back on the shelf. "Dora can't get upset over four cookies." He took a generous bite, then led her out again.

Dora stood at the stove, her spoon still in hand, and waved it at Oliver again. "I take it you left some?"

"We each took two," he said in exasperation.

She smiled at Etta. "Did he?"

She held hers up. "Yes."

He took another bite and nodded.

Etta smiled. Oliver Darling was just that, darling. But the name change still bothered her. If they didn't use their real last name, had there been other things they told the people of Apple Blossom that weren't quite the truth? And if so, had they fessed up to their future brides?

"Come, let's step out back," Oliver suggested. He took her elbow and steered her toward the door leading to the hall. They exited out a back door and now stood behind the hotel.

"I never come back here," she said. "It's pretty."

"Yes, with the orchards and green grass – a lovely picnic spot." He motioned to the grassy ground. "Shall we?"

She smiled as he took her hand and helped her sit. "Thank you."

Oliver smiled as he sat next to her. "You're quite welcome." He began to munch on his second cookie.

Etta watched him for a moment and noted the square of his jaw, the thickness of his dark hair. Like the rest of the Darlings, he was handsome, but she hadn't noticed how much until now. Her heart quickened, and she had to look away. *No, no, no.* She didn't dare let her attraction grow. Of all the Darlings, Oliver was the one that would leave Apple Blossom and probably never return. Not after what happened today. His mother would marry him off the first chance she got, from the sound of it.

Her heart sank and she tried to think of something else. "About the plumbing. How much do you think putting in the proper plumbing would cost?"

"I'm not sure. We'll have to ask the captain. He knows more about this sort of thing than the rest of us. Mr. McSweeney might also have a good idea."

"I haven't seen him all day."

Oliver took a deep breath and smiled. "I think he ran for cover the moment he heard my mother in the lobby."

She forced a smile. "I'm sorry for you."

His face fell. "Why?"

"To have such a horrible woman for a mother. I'd give anything to have a mother."

He straightened on the grass. "Etta, I'm sorry. I know we talk about her as if she's some horrid fire-breathing beast, but she means well."

"Does she?"

He sighed. "She just has different ideas as to what we consider our best interest. Sterling and the others see nothing wrong with falling in love with an American. So long as the young lady is kind, of good moral character, and values the same things we do, then let the weddings begin." He looked at the orchards and sighed again. "Once we have a preacher, that is."

"There's always Virginia City."

"True, but Sterling was hoping multiple weddings to

start a new preacher off in Apple Blossom would help convince him to stay. My brothers plan to marry all at once. Wouldn't that be something?"

Etta had noticed Letty and Cassie coming out of Alma's with ivory fabric one day. They had started on their wedding dresses. The longer it took for a preacher to come to town, the longer they had to work on them. "Yes," she finally said. "It would."

Oliver raised his face to the sky and closed his eyes. "I will miss the weather here."

"Is it so different from England?"

"Oh, quite. But I won't miss the mosquitoes." He slapped at his neck.

Her heart went out to him. He looked troubled and she wondered if he knew his burdens showed. "I hope you'll be happy when you get home."

He looked at her. "Thank you, Etta. I wish you much happiness too."

She smiled as her heart sank. She didn't want him to go. Now that she'd taken notice, she realized what a shame it was that he was leaving.

They sat in silence for a time and watched the clouds roll by. It was lovely, and she didn't know sharing a quiet moment with someone could make her so at peace. Would she ever have moments like this again? She munched on her cookies, wiped her hands on the grassy ground, then lay on her back.

"What are you doing?" Oliver asked.

"What does it look like?" She laced her fingers behind her head and stared at the sky. "Look, I see a squirrel."

He repositioned himself and lay next to her. "Where?"

She glanced at him as she blushed. "There." She pointed. "Next to the big fat cloud." She cocked her head and peered at it. "That one looks a little like the captain."

Oliver laughed. "Don't let him hear you say that. Personally, I think it looks like the barber in the village."

"In England?"

"Mm-hmm." He looked at her and smiled. "I've never looked at clouds with someone before."

She looked at him. "Never?"

"I'm afraid not." He studied the sky. "See that thinner cloud with the funny little bump at one end?"

"Yes."

"That looks like my Aunt Paulette."

Etta snorted with laughter.

"No, really. You should see the size of her nose..."

She laughed harder and saw him smiling out the corner of one eye. "And is she really that thin?"

"Oh, yes. And can rival my mother in trying to get her way." He looked at her and cringed. "You should see what they're like when they're together. It's frightening."

She laughed. Unfortunately, after what little she'd seen of his mother, she didn't want to think about it.

"I suppose we should go inside." He smiled as he sat up. "Did you need something more to eat?"

"No, I'm fine. Thank you." She sat up too. "Oliver?"

He offered her his hand. She took it and he pulled her to her feet. "Yes?"

Etta gazed into his eyes, curious what she might see in their depths. "Are you ever coming back to Apple Blossom?"

His face fell for a moment, then he plastered on a smile. "Of course. My brothers are here."

She bit her lip as her heart leaped in her chest. "But will you stay?"

He locked gazes with her. "I cannot say."

Etta smiled ruefully, not caring if he read it for what it was. She nodded in resignation and headed for the hotel's back door.

Oliver watched Etta go ahead of him and had a sudden vision of the two of them dancing at a ball. She would be beautiful in a gown of silver and blue. The colors would set off her eyes and her dark hair. Men would no doubt ask after her and try to find out who she was. A daughter of a baron, perhaps? Maybe a count? He got a sour taste in his mouth thinking of those same imaginary suitors when they found out she was a blacksmith from Apple Blossom.

Instead of heading into the dining room, Etta cut into the kitchen, Oliver on her heels. "Do you need any help?" she asked Dora.

Dora looked around the kitchen. "No, Jean and I

have everything in hand. Why don't you take a seat in the dining room and enjoy your evening?"

Etta turned to him. "Will your parents be joining us?"

He looked apologetic. "I'm afraid so."

She sighed, then crossed the kitchen to the door leading to the dining room.

"She's braver than we are," Jean commented as he followed.

He stopped at the door and faced them. "Perhaps, but Etta isn't the one my mother will complain about the food to." He saluted them, then left. He shouldn't have done that. For all he knew, Mother would love fried chicken. But there were no guarantees, and he didn't want them to delude themselves into thinking Mother would let them get through the evening unscathed. She would say something. It was her way.

Etta sat at a small table on the other side of the room. Oliver joined her. "What are you doing way over here? We usually occupy the large center table."

"There won't be enough room with your parents here. Besides, I would imagine your brothers will all bring their future wives to dinner."

"Oh, yes, you're quite right." He sat across from her and smiled. "This is cozy."

"But will it be peaceful?"

"One can only hope." His eyes flicked to the lobby as Irving, Sarah, and her children entered the dining room. They took one look at Oliver, then took their usual places at the large center table while Irving sauntered over. "Planning to dine off the battlefield?" he commented.

"Well, I'm not betrothed like the rest of you."

"Ah, but you are sitting with a beautiful young woman. Mother is bound to think you are."

Etta blushed and looked away.

Oliver gave Irving a look that clearly said, *nice going*, then glanced at the lobby. Letty and Sterling were entering the dining room, followed by Wallis. The latter went straight to the kitchen. Phileas came out the kitchen door, said a few words to Wallis, then also entered the room. "Ah, I see almost all of us are... Oliver, what are you and Etta doing way over there?"

"Sitting," he called back.

Etta blushed again and sank a little in her chair. "Maybe I should leave."

"Nonsense," Sterling said as he approached their table. "There's no reason you can't sit over here."

"Can we sit with them?" Flint asked from the big table.

Now Oliver blushed. "Then the only thing missing would be Nanny Geary."

Phileas snorted. "Father would find that amusing."

"Mother, not so much." Sterling surveyed the dining room. "Where arc Conrad and Cassie?"

"I'm sure they'll be along," Wallis said as he joined them. "A better question is, where are Mother and Father?"

"Right here."

Everyone turned at the sound of their mother's voice. She entered the dining room on Father's arm, head held high, looking down her nose at Letty, Sarah and the children seated around the large table. "Well, don't just stand there, Sterling, who are these people?"

Oliver saw his eldest brother's jaw tighten. "Sit, Mother," Sterling said. "I'll introduce you." He motioned the others to the center table, then glanced over his shoulder at Oliver and Etta. "You two stay where you are," he said in a low voice. "This is our fight and there's no sense dragging you into it."

"But Sterling...," Oliver began.

Sterling held up a hand to silence him and continued to the other table.

Etta leaned his way. "Oliver, are you sure we should?"

He mustered up a smile for her. "It's for the best."

She leaned a little closer. "Will your parents think that we... I mean..."

"Are together?" He sighed. "Let them think what they want. My mother has to learn she can't always have things her way."

"Oliver," Mother snapped. "What are you doing over there?"

He shrugged. "Sitting."

"Come here at once."

He glanced at Etta and back. "No. There's no need as there's no room."

"One of these women can sit with..." She peered at Etta. "Who is that?"

Oliver stood, gave Etta a slight bow, then faced his mother. "Miss Etta Whitehead. She and I will dine together this evening." With that he retook his seat as the hotel's other guests filed into the room. The five strangers would take up two more tables, leaving only one left in a corner. If Conrad was smart, he'd take it when he and Cassie arrived. He wondered if Jean and Dora would opt to eat in the kitchen. But they'd have to face his parents at some point tonight; it might as well be during the evening meal.

"Where's the food?" the youngest of the strangers— Jonny, was it?—whined.

"It'll come," Frank said, eyeing the big table. Oliver watched his eyes settle on Mother and winced. He hoped and prayed she didn't start speaking to them or there would be trouble.

"I'm hungry," said another of the men.

Oliver was about to go check to see if Dora was ready to bring the food out when Cassie came through the kitchen door carrying a large platter of fried chicken, Conrad on her heels. She went straight to the large table, set it down, then smiled at the men seated at the other two tables. "Yours is coming, gentlemen." She turned and headed for the kitchen door.

"Great Scott," Father said. "Was she wearing a gun and a lawman's star?"

"What?" Frank said, his head snapping to the kitchen door.

"She was," Conrad said. "That was Sheriff Cassie Laine, my betrothed."

The five men gaped at him.

So did Mother. "Your betrothed?" Her eyes fixed on the deputy's star on his vest. "What is that?"

Conrad grinned. "Did I fail to mention that I'm the town deputy?"

Father gasped. Mother gasped louder.

Oliver wanted to hide under the table, but he was no coward. He'd help his brothers if he thought they needed it. But he began to wonder how they'd survive the evening.

Chapter Eleven

Etta watched Oliver's mother's face go red as a beet. "Conrad," she hissed. "What do you think you're doing?"

He glanced at his brothers seated around the table. "Working," he finally said. "I have a job."

His mother's jaw dropped. "You're... working?!"

"Yes. What's wrong with that?"

His mother's hand flew to her chest. "Charles, don't just sit there, do something!"

Mr. Darlington eyed his son. "I hope you're proficient enough with a gun to handle a job like that."

"Charles!" Mrs. Darlington screeched and stood. She marched around the table to Conrad, grabbed the star and, after a tug or two, pulled it off his vest. "I won't have it, do you understand me? I won't!"

Sheriff Cassie stood poised in the kitchen's doorway, two plates of fried chicken in her hands. She scurried across the room and set one down at the table with two men, the other on the table with three. The strangers all exchanged a look of shock and embarrassment as they gaped at Mrs. Darlington.

"Oh, crumbs," Etta heard Oliver mutter under his breath.

Conrad looked at the deputy's star in his mother's hand. "Why did you do that?"

His mother laughed. "Why do you think? Where did you ever get the notion to do such a foolish thing? These people don't need you as their deputy. This town is ridiculous enough as it is." She spun on Cassie. "Just look at her. She's the sheriff? What does that tell you? That there's nothing here. No future, no hope, no chance to make something of yourself."

She turned to Conrad again. "And you think you're in love with her, do you?" she scoffed. "Ha! You're in love with all women and the sooner she gets that through her silly head the better." She gave Cassie a hard stare then returned to her chair. Mr. Darlington stood to help her with it, and as soon as she was settled, retook his own seat.

So Oliver's mother was what Agnes would be like with more position and power. Etta shuddered at the thought.

"And you." Mrs. Darlington fixed her eyes on Sterling. "What's her story? Dressmaker? Cook? Farmer's daughter?"

Sterling's jaw tightened. From the look of it he was

seething, yet stayed perfectly still, his voice even. "Letty Henderson owns and operates a ranch outside of town. She provides milk to the community as many folks here don't own a cow."

Mrs. Darlington laughed. "A milkmaid. How quaint." Her eyes fell on Wallis next. "And what about you?"

He took a deep breath. "If you must know, I'm betrothed to the town undertaker."

Mr. Darlington's jaw dropped this time. "What?"

"Yes, the undertaker," Wallis said calmly. "She also runs the local library."

"Of course she does," their mother spat. She looked at Phileas. "Go on, get it over with."

"Dora is the most wonderful, beautiful woman in the world to me, Mother. And frankly, after watching your behavior this evening, I'm rethinking our plan to help you and Father out."

"Help us?" she snapped. "With what?" She shook her head in disgust and turned to Irving. She gave him what Etta decided must be her signature hard stare, then looked at Sarah, Flint and Lacey. The latter began to cry.

Irving stood. "That does it. Sarah, children, we're leaving."

Sarah couldn't get out of her chair fast enough and made sure Flint and Lacey were quick to comply. "Come along, children. We're going home."

"But what about dinner?" Flint whined.

Sarah steered them toward the kitchen instead of the lobby and Jean followed them inside.

Oliver closed his eyes a moment, opened them, then got to his feet. "Mother..."

"Sit down, Oliver. You're the only one in the room with any sense."

He approached the big table and stopped, facing her. Etta held her breath for whatever might happen next. "You've come here because you received a telegraph message from a gossip who can't keep her nose out of other people's business. You show up here without question on the word of someone you don't even know. That you did tells me you don't know us."

Mrs. Darlington slowly got to her feet. "Now hear this, Oliver. You will pack your bags and return to England with us. There I will groom you for the role of viscount, taking over for your father once he passes. Is that understood?"

He straightened. "And if I don't?"

"Then none of you gets a penny. I will not only see that the lot of you are disinherited, but you will never set foot on the estate again, is that understood?"

Etta couldn't see if Oliver was looking at Sterling or not. He took a deep breath. "Perfectly." He returned to his seat, and she could see he was mad as a rattler.

"Oliver," she whispered.

He held up his hand, his jaw set. "Not now, Etta."

She sat back, her chest burning with helplessness. She hated a bully. Pa had been one, especially when he was drunk. Unable to help herself, she stood, marched over to Mr. and Mrs. Darlington and frowned. "You disgust me."

Mrs. Darlington's jaw slacked. "Who are you?" She gasped. "Don't tell me you and Oliver...?"

Etta didn't know why she said what she did, but out it came. "So what if we are?" She marched back to her table, pulled Oliver to his feet and kissed him square on the mouth.

Etta didn't realize she'd closed her eyes until they opened, and she saw Oliver's popped wide.

"Woo-ee!" one stranger whooped. "That was somethin'!"

She didn't know which one said it and didn't care. She was so fired up she could spit in Mrs. Darlington's face. What a horrible, horrible woman. And she wasn't the only one. Agnes did this. All this upset was her fault.

"Etta..."

She looked at Oliver, realized she was still holding onto the lapels of his jacket and let go. "I'm sorry," she whispered.

"Hey, uh, someone?" Frank called. "Can we get some service here?"

Etta sighed and marched to the kitchen door. She burst in, stopped, and looked around. Dora was fixing plates for Sarah and the children while Jean stood against the wall, wide-eyed. "Mashed potatoes," Etta said. "The men want their food."

Jean nodded and headed for the stove. She handed Etta two bowls of potatoes, then grabbed two bowls of green beans and started for the kitchen door. Etta followed, and they served the strangers, then went back for more. Irving, Sarah and the children, each with a plate in their hands, made for the opposite door to the hallway. They were probably going up the street to their future home to eat.

Etta grabbed two more bowls of mashed potatoes and went into the dining room. Everyone was stone-faced including Mr. and Mrs. Darlington, who were looking around at the others as if they were about to be in a gunfight. She set the bowls on the table, plopping one in front of Mrs. Darlington.

"And what are you?" the woman asked. "The town laundress?"

"No, ma'am. That would be Sarah Crawford, Irving's betrothed." Etta grinned. "I'm the blacksmith." She spun on her heel and went back to the kitchen for more food. Let the woman chew on that.

When she entered the kitchen this time, she stopped to take a breath. Good grief! Did she just do and say those things? She'd always wanted to stand up to Pa like that but never had the guts. Instead she remained silent, hid, and hoped for the best.

Etta took a few deep breaths to calm herself. Staying upset would not help things and she hoped she just hadn't made things worse.

"Are you okay?" Dora asked.

Etta gave her a blank stare, then remembered something else she did. "Merciful heavens. I kissed Oliver!"

Oliver stood, dumbfounded, and watched Etta bring food to the different tables. Every one's but his. But that was okay—he was still in shock over her kiss, and though it wasn't the sort of kiss to strike passion in a man, it was still a bold thing for her to do. His admiration for her went up ten notches. She'd stood up to Mother, and that said a lot.

Jean came into the dining room, followed by Dora and Etta, and brought food to his table. She smiled at him as she set down a plate of chicken. "Etta just told me what she did."

He nodded, still speechless.

"We're all standing our ground," she added in a low voice.

Oliver nodded again. "Steady on, then."

She nodded back as Dora approached with two bowls, one of potatoes, the other vegetables. She set them down, winked, then straightened her shoulders and went to the big table, taking her usual place next to Phileas.

Jean sat next to Wallis. "Are we staying?"

"Yes," Wallis said. "We'll not waste your hard work."

"This is right fine chicken!" Frank called from his table. "My compliments."

Mother rolled her eyes and peered at the platter of

chicken before her. Perhaps she'd given up for now and was hungry. She and Father had a long journey and, with any luck, would eat and retire for the evening. Tomorrow was another day. Etta may have won them the battle this evening and shut Mother up for now, but it wasn't going to last.

Etta rejoined him and sat. "I'm starving."

Before he could say anything, Phileas said the blessing and the rest of them began to eat.

Oliver looked at Etta and smiled, feeling a sense of relief wash over him. Even though the tension in the room was still palpable, there was a newfound sense of camaraderie among them. Etta had taken a bold step, and her actions no doubt had given everyone a new respect for her. Save his parents, of course.

He watched Etta take a bite of chicken and couldn't help but notice the way her lips wrapped around the meat, or how her tongue darted out to catch the juices. It made him realize just how hungry he was.

He reached for a piece of chicken and took a bite, savoring the flavors. But his eyes never left Etta as she ate. He wondered what it would be like to taste those lips again, this time with more passion.

As if sensing his thoughts, she smiled knowingly and took another bite of chicken. But this time, she didn't swallow right away. Her cheeks were flushed, and her gaze kept darting up to meet his before quickly dropping back to her plate. He couldn't help but smile at her shyness. She must be embarrassed by her earlier actions.

"It's okay," he said softly, breaking the silence between them.

Etta looked up, her eyes meeting his for a moment before she glanced away again. "Yes, everything's fine," she breathed.

Oliver leaned closer to her, his voice low and intimate. "You know, you don't have to be nervous around me," he said. "Especially not after... well, you were magnificent."

"I-I don't know what to say," she stammered, her eyes flicking up to meet his again.

Oliver reached across the table and took her hand in his, his thumb stroking her knuckles in a comforting gesture. "You don't need to say anything. I'm sure I speak for my brothers and me when I say, bravo." He waited for her to say something, but she didn't. Still, he now had a sense of belonging, and for the first time since coming to Apple Blossom felt like he was part of something bigger than himself. He realized he'd been so focused on his own problems that he'd forgotten there were other people who cared about him and wanted to help him.

Everyone ate in silence, and he was surprised his parents didn't take their food and eat in their room. If he knew his mother, she was plotting on how to get his brothers to come back to England and leave their future brides behind. But that wasn't about to happen.

As they finished their meal, Dora came over to their table. "Would you like some dessert?" she asked, holding out a plate of cookies.

Oliver looked at Etta, who nodded eagerly. "Yes, please!" she said, grinning. He knew she was remembering their earlier venture into the larder and raiding the cookie jar.

Dora set the plate in front of Oliver. "Enjoy!" she said before heading back to the kitchen.

Oliver took a bite of cookie, savoring the sweet flavor. As he chewed, a sense of gratitude washed over him. He was grateful for the food, for the company, for he and his siblings standing up to Mother, and for Etta, who shyly munched on a cookie and stole glances at him the entire time.

"That was mighty fine," Frank said across the room and patted his belly.

"It sure was," one of his dinner companions agreed. Herbert, was it? Oliver couldn't remember.

"Yep, the food was great and the entertainment too!" the youngest chortled.

Mother frowned but said nothing.

"I ain't had this much fun since that saloon in Abilene," another said. Was it the cousin? Oliver couldn't think of his name either.

"Yeah, this was better than watching a bar fight!" said another.

Etta giggled at his remark, and Oliver slowly grinned at her. He was glad to see her loosening up and enjoying herself. It was a rare sight, and he was grateful for it, despite the circumstances.

As they finished their cookies, Mother and Father

stood up from their table. "We'll be retiring for the evening," Mother announced stiffly. "Goodnight."

"Goodnight, Mother," Oliver said, his voice polite but distant.

She gave him her usual glare. "Come along, Charles."

"Goodnight, Father," Oliver added.

His brothers said nothing, still too mad to speak.

Oliver watched his parents leave the room, their footsteps echoing in the silence that followed. He knew this was only the beginning of the battle, but for now he was content to enjoy the moment and the newfound camaraderie among them.

"Well, that was interesting," Wallis said, breaking the silence. "I'm glad we stood our ground."

"Me too," Jean agreed. "I was afraid your mother would never stop."

"And I'm glad we have Etta on our side," Phileas added with a smile. He turned in his chair to face her. "She's a force to be reckoned with."

Etta blushed at the compliment, but Oliver could see the pride in her eyes. She had done something brave and important, and it had earned her the respect of his siblings.

"I'm turnin' in," Frank said. He stood and shook his head. "Tarnation, ya got a big problem on yer hands. Good luck to ya." He put on his hat and headed for the lobby. His friends followed, chuckling amongst themselves at their plight.

Oliver leaned back in his chair and let out a

contented sigh. "I have to admit, that went better than I expected."

Etta gaped at him. "Better.?"

He smiled back at her. "Thanks to you. And we appreciate it. More than you know."

Etta's expression softened. "I meant what I said to your mother, Oliver," she said. "But I'm not sure how much help it was. Maybe all I did was add fuel to the fire, but I had to say something. She was being so awful to you."

Oliver felt a warmth spread through him at her words. "Thank you," he said softly.

They sat in silence for a few moments, just enjoying each other's company. It was nice having Etta by his side this evening. She was brave, kind and fiercely loyal. He couldn't imagine going through this without her.

As the clock struck eight, Jean yawned and stood up from the table. "I don't know about you, but I need to get some sleep after all that. Dora, I'll help you with the dishes first."

As everyone rose from their tables and cleared the dishes, Oliver had a sense of relief. They had won this battle, but there would be more to come. He knew his parents wouldn't give up. Though Mother blasted them like cannon fire, Father would have his own thoughts— some in their favor, some not. He was quiet, and would hit them individually like a sniper in the grass. If Oliver's guess was right, he'd start with Sterling and Letty.

Chapter Twelve

Etta tossed and turned all night. She was still thinking about kissing Oliver. He said it was all right, and brave. But that's not what she thought. To her it was a stupid thing to do, and only made his mother so mad she shut up. What else could it be? She'd seen Agnes upset enough to know how that type of person reacted to things. They always had to get in the last word and could cut you down without blinking an eye. Maybe she *had* made things worse for Oliver.

Then again, maybe he was right, and it was the right thing to do, but she couldn't shake off the feeling of regret. She'd crossed a line, and now things would never be the same. For one, now she'd have to fight. She'd entered the battle when she spoke up and then kissed him. His mother would be out to get her as much as the others.

As the night wore on, her thoughts turned to Oliver himself. There was no denying she was attracted to him, but she didn't want to complicate things. They were already dealing with enough as it was. She sighed and turned over, staring at the ceiling. Maybe she should try to ignore her feelings and focus on helping Oliver and his siblings. That was the most important thing right now.

She left her cot, walked to the only window, and looked out at the moonlit clearing. It was quiet outside, the only sound the crickets chirping in the bushes. She sighed and leaned her forehead against the cool glass. What had she gotten herself into?

Well, there was no use lamenting over her actions. She might as well try to get some sleep. It didn't come easy. By the time the first rays of sunlight filtered through the window, she gave up, dressed quickly and left her room, hoping to get some fresh air and clear her head. She walked around to the back of the livery stable, trying to shake off the feeling of unease now settled in her stomach.

She wished the town had a preacher—then Oliver's brothers could marry and that would be that. But so long as they weren't, their mother would try to pry them away from their betrothed and Apple Blossom. The question was, how far would she go? Was she joking last night about disinheriting them? And from what? How big was their farm?

She decided she'd better feed the horses and returned

to the livery stable. Once there she pulled hay from a bale, put it in a wheelbarrow, then took it to the corral.

As she walked, she heard footsteps behind her and turned, expecting to see Oliver, but instead saw one of the strangers. If her guess was right, he was one of the three brothers. The middle one, maybe?

"Morning," he said, smiling at her. "I saw you and thought I'd join you, if that's all right. I wanted to check on the horses."

Etta nodded, unsure what to say.

"It's a beautiful morning, ain't it?" He gestured to the sky. "Name's Dale. I always find a walk in the fresh air helps clear my head. 'Specially when there's so much going on."

Etta nodded again, still not sure if she should say anything. Heck, she still felt guilty about kissing Oliver, and didn't want to talk about it with a stranger. She hoped he didn't bring it up. To this man and his cohorts, the fight between the Darlings was nothing more than a form of entertainment.

"That was sure something last night," Dale said, his tone serious. "It was also pretty brave standing up to that old crow. In fact, it was downright admirable."

Etta gave him a blank stare. "Um, thank you."

He smiled. "Yep, she's a wily one. You wouldn't know when she's leaving, do you?"

"Not soon enough for me." She opened the gate and wheeled the hay into the corral.

Dale followed and began distributing flakes to the

horses. "Where's your pa? I'm thinking he should look at our horses before we head out. I think their shoes are okay, but you never know."

Etta closed her eyes a moment. She was going to have to say something. "He's... not here. But I can look at them for you. I help run the shop."

"You?" he said with raised eyebrows. "But you're just a little thing."

Her hand went to her hip. "And perfectly capable of shoeing a horse. I'll take care of it." She tossed the last flake of hay to the horses, took the wheelbarrow and headed for the gate.

Dale chuckled. "All right, all right, I meant nothing by it. Just curious, is all."

Etta nodded, feeling self-conscious. She opened the gate and pushed the wheelbarrow out of the corral.

Dale followed her, still looking somewhat surprised. "Well, I'll be. I guess appearances can deceive," he said with a chuckle. "I'll help you with the horses, then."

Etta smiled tightly. She didn't particularly like Dale, but she knew she needed to be civil. "Sure, that would be great."

As they walked back to the livery stable, Etta was a little uneasy. She wondered what his true intentions were. Was he just trying to be friendly, or was there something more? She pushed the thought aside as they entered the stable and, after putting the wheelbarrow away, she gathered what she needed to check the horses.

Dale prattled on about different horses he'd owned

over the years, then out of the blue, asked about Agnes. "So, is she a nice woman, the banker's wife? She ain't all uppity like that Englishwoman, is she?"

"Why do you ask?"

"On account my brother and cousin had a run-in with her yesterday. They ain't sure which is worse, that banker's wife or that harpy from last night. Speaking of which, what do you think'll happen now?"

Etta shrugged. "I don't know. I hope things calm down, but I have a feeling they won't."

He nodded. "Yeah, I have a feeling you're right. Mothers can be... difficult. But if'n you ask me, fathers are the real problem. I noticed them boys' father was quiet, but I bet he's smart. He knows how to get what he wants."

Etta didn't like the sound of that. She had a feeling things were only going to get worse. "Well, we'll just have to be prepared for whatever comes our way."

Dale nodded in agreement, then gazed her. "You know, you and that Oliver fella make a good team."

Etta's heart skipped a beat. "Excuse me?"

"He's a fancy Englishman and you're a smart, capable woman. I don't know why you're wasting your time in a place like this. You could do much more with your life."

Etta frowned, not liking the direction this conversation was heading. "What do you mean?"

"I mean, you could be in the city, making something of yourself. Instead, you're stuck here in this little town, working in a blacksmith's shop of all places. It's a shame, really."

Etta narrowed her eyes, feeling defensive. "I like it here. I enjoy helping people and working with my hands."

"But there's so much more out there for you," Dale persisted. He glanced toward the hotel. "Take my brother Jonny. He's a little rough around the edges, but a fella like him would do you good."

She sighed, grabbed a hoof pick, lead rope and halter, and headed back to the corral.

Dale followed, regaling her with his brothers exploits. Etta listened politely, but her mind was elsewhere. She couldn't shake the feeling that something was going to go wrong. She didn't know what was, but she had a sense of impending doom. She didn't want to alarm Dale, so she kept her thoughts to herself.

When they reached the corral, she caught the first horse she came to, had Dale hold onto the lead rope, then grabbed the hoof pick from her apron pocket and began checking the horse's hooves.

Dale stood by, watching her work. "You're good at this," he said admiringly.

Etta smiled, feeling a bit more at ease. "Thank you. My pa taught me when I was young."

He nodded, still watching her work. "I wish I'd had someone like that to teach me. I had to learn everything on my own. Well, Herbert, he's my big brother, he helped. When he felt like it."

Etta had a pang of sympathy for him. She knew what it was like to fend for oneself. "It's difficult, but it can be done. You just have to put in the work."

"Work," he said in disgust. "But I suppose if'n you like the work you do, then it's okay."

She put the horse's hoof down and straightened. "And do you like the work you do?"

He grinned ear to ear. "Oh, missy, you have no idea."

Oliver didn't sleep well and yawned on his way down to breakfast. Maybe he should opt to eat in the kitchen so he wouldn't have to speak to his parents... oh. Too late—they were already seated at the large table. He sighed and entered the dining room. "Morning, Mother, Father." He glanced at the table he and Etta occupied the night before and his chest warmed. It was hard not to think about their kiss last night after he walked her home.

"Well, don't just stand there,' Mother snapped. "Sit. I'd like to talk to you before your brothers arrive."

"If they arrive," Father added dryly.

"They get hungry enough, they will," she countered.

Oliver sat in his usual chair and eyed the bowl of muffins already on the table. "What would you like to say, Mother?" He grabbed one and reached for the crock of butter.

"How did this happen? I thought I raised you better than this."

He looked at her and sighed. "Mother, Sterling and the others fell in love. How does it usually happen?"

"With contracts, a bit of courting if there's time, and then over time, of course."

Dora entered the dining room with a large platter of fried potatoes and set it on the table. Without a word, she retreated to the kitchen.

"Rather sullen, isn't she?" Father commented.

"After your behavior last night, do you blame her? Don't expect many warm greetings this morning." Oliver took a large bite of muffin. He hoped Dora brought the coffee next.

"My behavior was justified," Mother insisted. "The six of you shocked me. I told your father letting you come to America by yourselves was a bad idea."

"Now, Cordelia," Father said. "Young men have to sow their wild oats, as they say. I thought the trip would be good for them."

"And so it was," Oliver said. 'They all fell in love."

"Did you?" Mother asked.

Part of him didn't want to answer. "Not yet."

She gasped. "Don't you dare, Oliver. Not if you know what's good for you. Your brothers might be lost to us, but at least you're still in your right mind."

He sighed again. "Mother, if I were to fall in love, then I'd marry the girl."

"You're not allowed to fall in love here, only in England and to a young lady of good breeding and a wealthy family."

He rolled his eyes, not caring if it was disrespectful.

"If you're not in love, then why did that young woman kiss you?" Father asked.

Olive stared at him and realized how tired he was. That kiss kept him up half the night. "That's Etta for you," he finally said.

"Hmph, knew it," Mother said. "A loose woman. I bet the town is full of them."

Oliver pinched the bridge of his nose as Dora brought the coffee pot and a plate of bacon. She poured Oliver a cup, then left the pot on the table.

Mother gaped at her as she left. "How rude."

"As were you last night, Mother." Oliver shoved the pot toward her. "Pour yourself some."

"Allow me, dear." Father picked up the pot, filled her cup, then his own. "Tell me, boy, are your brothers truly set on marrying these women?"

"As I said, they're in love."

"But you're not?"

"Father..." He thought of Etta's kiss, her bravery, and the way her whole body trembled when she gave Mother what for. "Who knows?"

"What?!" Mother spat. "Say it isn't so."

"Why? Are you going to disinherit the lot of us and have no one to leave your vast estate to? What about grandchildren? Do you honestly plan on never meeting them? We had a plan, you know. A good plan that would make everybody happy, even you, Mother."

He dished himself a plate, not caring that he wasn't

waiting for his brothers to come down. If they came down. For all he knew, none of them were in the hotel. Sterling may have gone to Letty's, Irving was probably at his building up the street. Conrad might be at Cassie's, and Wallis was probably hunkered down in the funeral parlor. Each would have a lovely breakfast of some sort with their intended while he was stuck with their parents. He said a silent blessing over his food and began to eat.

Father began spooning potatoes onto his plate as Dora brought a plate of fried eggs out. "Oliver, I'll be in the kitchen if you need me."

He eyed the kitchen door. Phileas was probably having his breakfast in there, out of sight of their parents. "Thank you, Dora."

"Dora," Mother repeated. "You own this establishment?"

"I do." Dora stood, looking stern. "Now if you'll excuse me?" She turned on her heel and left.

Mother stared after her with a pinched look that reminded Oliver of Agnes. Speaking of which, had anyone spoken to her yet? He might after breakfast. All of this was her fault.

Mother served herself and didn't look happy about it. She liked being waited on hand and foot, but considering how much traveling she'd done to get here, was probably growing used to having to do some things for herself.

They ate in silence and Oliver was beginning to suspect that his brothers would regroup this morning and preparing for another battle later in the day. Maybe

143

he could help by disarming Mother beforehand. He sipped his coffee then reached for the pot. "You can't always get what you want, you know."

Father laughed. "On the contrary, boy. Your mother always gets what she wants."

Oliver poured himself more coffee. "Even if it means making your sons miserable for the rest of their lives?"

Mother looked at him. "What do you mean?"

Oliver leaned toward her. "They. Are. In. Love." He sat back and picked up his cup. "Take that away from them, and they will hate you. Is that what you want? Because that's what you'll get by trying to bend them to your will."

"We'll disinherit them," she stated calmly.

"They don't care, Mother. *Love* doesn't care about money or estates or titles."

"It should," she spat, then stabbed at her eggs.

He sighed in frustration. There was no getting through that thick skull of hers. She was set on he and his brothers marrying ladies from the aristocracy and that was that. "Well, then it's too bad this will be the last time you see any of us."

She stopped, a forkful of eggs halfway to her mouth. "What do you mean? You're coming home with us."

He shook his head. "No. I'm not."

"But you're not in love," Father huffed.

"Perhaps not, but I know right from wrong. And this—" He pointed at the table. "—is so wrong it hurts." He tossed his napkin onto the table, rose from his chair, and left the dining room before either of his parents could say another word. They were being ridiculous and stubborn.

He left the hotel, marched across the street, and realized he was heading to the livery stable. Fine, he could do with a visit with Etta. Maybe being with her would calm his nerves. He was so frazzled his skin itched. He hoped he wasn't breaking out in hives!

He entered the blacksmith's shop and looked around. There was no sign of Etta. Maybe she was cleaning stalls. He went into the livery stable next door and searched, but there was no sign of her there either. He finally found her in the corral with one of the men passing through, checking a horse.

"And then you should've seen what Jonny did next," the man said with a laugh. "He done shot himself in the foot!" He flew into hysterics.

Etta sighed impatiently. "How unfortunate," she said dryly.

"Good morning," Oliver interjected. "Am I disturbing you?"

She looked relieved. "Not at all."

Oliver smiled at the man. "Dale, isn't it?"

"Yeah, so?"

Oliver nodded. "Sorry about last night, old chap. That was something no one should have to witness."

Dale shrugged. "I'm glad she ain't my mother." He turned to Etta. "All done?"

"Yes, they're all fine. You could ride out today." She

145

glanced at Oliver, and he caught the hopefulness in her eyes.

"We plan to as soon as we get a few more supplies. Thank you kindly." Dale tipped his hat, handed Etta the lead rope and left the corral.

She smiled in relief. "Thank goodness they're leaving."

Oliver watched Dale head back to the hotel. "Yes. Now if only my parents would too." He looked at her and sighed. "But that's not about to happen. There's too much to fix now."

Chapter Thirteen

Etta saw the forlorn look on Oliver's face. "You regret what you said to them last night?"

"No. But perhaps a little of what I said this morning."

Her heart went out to him. "I'm sorry, Oliver. I wish there was more that I could do. I hope what I did last night didn't hurt things."

He laughed. "Oh, Etta, there's nothing you could have done to add any more. My mother is determined to drag all of us back to England and will pull everything she has out of her hat to do so. But we won't go."

"Not even you?' She caught the hint of hopefulness in her voice, and hoped he didn't.

"Not after this." He headed for the gate. "You're all done here?"

"Yes." She gathered the lead rope and halter.

"Would you like some breakfast?"

Her mouth watered at the thought. 'Where?"

"Hotel kitchen? It should be safe."

Her belly rumbled and she put her hand over it. "I wouldn't mind a bite."

"Jolly good." He offered her his arm and she took it without hesitation. They were allies now and she wanted to be close to him. She couldn't shake the feeling that something bad was going to happen. Maybe she was just upset from last night. Oliver's mother had done a good job of scattering the troops. She had seen no sign of Sterling, Conrad, Irving, Wallis or Phileas. Were they even in the hotel? "Um, how did breakfast go? Did you already have yours?"

"Yes, and no. I could have had more, but also couldn't stand to listen to my mother's ludicrous idea that we all must wed women of *her* choosing. She can't seem to get it through her head that my brothers are in love."

Etta went into her shop and hung up the halter and lead rope. "Maybe she's never been in love."

He leaned against a post. "Hmmm, perhaps you're right. My parents had an arranged marriage. But one would think they loved each other at some point. They had six children, after all."

She smiled. "Yes, they certainly did." She left the shop.

"What?" he asked, starting after her.

She waited for him to catch up. "I meant nothing by it. Your parents had six handsome sons, all of which are kindhearted, generous, hardworking and forthright. Who wouldn't fall in love with you?"

He looked her in the eyes as if to say, *have you?*

She swallowed and continued to the hotel. "Should we sneak in the back way?"

"Not necessary. My parents have probably retreated to their rooms. I just hope they're not giving poor Dora any grief."

"Was breakfast good?"

"Excellent as usual, from what I had."

When they reached the hotel, he opened the door for her and they went inside. She sighed in relief at the empty lobby and headed down the hall to the kitchen. The temptation to tiptoe was overwhelming, and she silently scolded herself for being a coward.

"Etta, Oliver," Dora called when they entered. "What are you doing here?"

"Etta's hungry," Oliver announced. "And I could do with a second helping. I know you have plenty."

"Yes, since your brothers and the others didn't come for breakfast." She went to the stove and took the lids off some frying pans. "At least the other hotel guests came down to eat. As soon as they did, you parents went to their rooms."

"Good," Oliver said. "One of the other guests might have insulted Mother and then she'd let him have it. At least this way bloodshed was avoided."

Dora turned to them in horror. "You don't think those men would shoot her, do you?"

"Them, shoot her?" Oliver said dryly. "Mother would eviscerate them with a fork."

Dora laughed. "Oh, my." She waved at the pans. "Help yourselves."

Etta took the plate Dora offered and went to the stove. She was starving. "One of them had me check their horses for loose shoes."

"And?" Dora said.

"They're all fine, and from the sounds of it they'll be leaving today."

Dora slumped against the dry sink. "Thank goodness."

Oliver took a plate and joined Etta at the stove. "I hope he got some breakfast. Can't ride out of town on an empty stomach."

"I'm just happy they're leaving," Dora said. "Now your parents can take a guest room and I can have my bed back."

Oliver grimaced. "You have the best rooms in the hotel, Dora. Mother's not likely to give them up."

Dora shook her head in dismay. "I almost wish the men would stay and your parents were the ones leaving. No offense."

He shrugged. "None taken." He filled his plate and followed Etta to the table.

She sat and waited for him to do the same. "Would you like to say the blessing?"

"Certainly." He clasped his hands before him and bowed his head. "Dear Lord, for what we are about to receive let us be truly thankful. And, um, on a side note, please seal my mother's mouth..."

"Oliver," Etta giggled.

He opened one eye and smiled at her. "All right, still her tongue, then. Amen."

Etta smiled. "I'm sorry."

He looked at her as he took a forkful of potatoes. "For what? And why are you smiling at me like that?"

"I'm sorry you have to put up with so much. No wonder none of you want to return to England."

He sighed. "Well, if not for Agnes, none of this would have happened. It would have been easier if Phileas, Dora and I went to England and explained things."

"What will you and your brothers do to Agnes?" Dora asked.

"Talk to her. There's not much else to do."

"You should let Agnes spend time with your mother. That would do the trick."

"Ha!" he laughed. "They might kill each other."

"Oh dear," Dora mused. "That wouldn't be good."

"Okay, perhaps a bit of maiming might occur. Either way, the two of them together would not be a good idea." He continued to eat.

Etta watched him for a moment, then pondered speaking to Agnes herself. Maybe if enough of them did, she'd think twice about sticking her nose so deeply into everyone else's business.

When they were done eating, they helped Dora with

the dishes and were about to leave when Oliver stopped at the door. "I say, but where is Phileas? I thought he'd be here in the kitchen with you."

"He went to Letty's to talk to Sterling. He spent the night out there."

"Hm. And Irving, Conrad, and Wallis?"

Dora crossed her arms. "None of them stayed here. Of course, that'll only make Agnes gossip more if she finds out."

He rubbed his face. "What a bother. Well, let's hope she doesn't." He opened the door and motioned Etta to precede him. She did and went straight for the hotel doors. She didn't want to chance a run-in with his parents, or the strangers for that matter. In fact, what she'd really like to do was head to the fishing hole. "Oliver?"

"Yes?"

She could hear the worry in his voice. "Would you like to go fishing with me?"

His eyes suddenly brightened. "I would."

She smiled. "I'm afraid I only have one fishing pole."

"That's fine by me. I'll watch you fish while I think."

"About what happened?"

"No, about how to make sure it doesn't happen again. This war is doing more than its share of damage, and I fear my mother's stubbornness will cause more of a rift between us."

She stopped them in the middle of the street. "I'm so sorry."

He looked into her eyes. "Don't be. None of this is your fault." He nodded at the blacksmith's shop. "Come along, let's get your pole and see if we catch anything. Maybe by the time we return, my brothers will have gathered and we'll go another round with the parents."

Etta's heart sank at the thought. Part of her was glad he wanted to stay, but if it was to spite his parents, then it wasn't right. The question was, how could she help mend something that was so broken?

They got Etta's pole and hurried up the street. Oliver had the same sense of exhilaration he used to get when he snuck off with his friends and missed school. He didn't do it often, but those rare times he had, made him feel like this. What if they got caught, how much trouble would they be in?

But he was no longer a schoolboy and Etta was not one of his classmates. She was a young woman that had stuck up for him and his brothers last night and delivered a blow to his parents by kissing him. Unfortunately, Mother now thought Etta was a loose woman. He was going to have to fix that and fast.

They saw no sign of Conrad or Cassie, nor did they see Irving, Sarah, or the children. Maybe they went to Sarah's house last night and Irving stayed there. It was, after all, not in town, and Mother had no idea where to look for them. He sighed when they left the road and started down the trail to the fishing spot.

"What's wrong?" Etta asked.

"You don't think we're being cowardly, do you?"

"How so?" She pushed a low-hanging branch aside as they passed.

"Avoiding my mother."

"Are you avoiding her?"

"I don't think so. I had breakfast with them. But it wasn't pleasant."

She stopped and turned to him. "Then you need this. It's amazing what a little peace and quiet will do for you."

Oliver tried not to look into her eyes and failed. She had the most beautiful eyes he'd ever seen. "Thank you. I needed to hear that."

"Your brothers are planning on coming to town, aren't they?" She smiled and started off again.

"Of course, and I assume they'll gather and knock on our parents' door."

"Should you be there?"

"Yes."

She stopped again. "We can turn around..."

"No, keep going. As you say, I need this."

She nodded knowingly and continued. By the time they reached the fishing hole, he was sweating. The day was already growing warm.

Etta went up a trail along the creek to the fishing spot and cast her line. That done, she sat on the grassy bank, a smile on her face.

"You like it here, don't you?"

"I do. I love everything about this spot. I always have. My pa used to bring me here all the time."

He laughed. "I thought this was supposed to be Billy's secret fishing hole."

"That everyone in town knows about, but Billy's one of the few that loves to fish. He comes in the afternoon, where I'll come late morning."

"So he doesn't run into you?"

She smiled. "No, because that's when the fish are still biting. His mother lets him fish in the afternoon when they aren't, then she doesn't have to cook the fish up for him."

He laughed. "I take it Mrs. Watson doesn't care for fish?"

"She does not." Etta braced her pole against a large rock and held it in place with a couple of smaller ones. As soon as she was done, she lay back in the grass with a sigh.

"You sound as if you're carrying the weight of the world on your shoulders," he said.

"No, just you." She gulped. "I mean..."

He smiled. "I appreciate your concern, Etta, I really do. But I don't want you to get too entangled in my family's sordid affairs."

"Sordid?"

Without thinking, he took her hand in his. "I don't want my mother aiming her anger at you. She's a sharp-tongued woman and skilled at tearing someone down. I've seen her do it more than once, but it was usually well deserved when it happened. Many times it was to protect us. But now that she's doing the same thing to us, it's quite different."

"Does she love you?"

Her question made him jerk. "I... yes. But she also loves her reputation, and I'm wondering which she loves more."

Etta shaded her eyes against the sun, and he noticed she didn't pull her hand from his. "Your mother sounds like she doesn't know either. Maybe she needs to be reminded which is more important. Your brothers are choosing their betrothed over reputation, from the sound of it. But I don't see why marrying American women would sully anyone's reputation."

He said nothing. Etta didn't know of their wealth or station and maybe it was best she didn't. He didn't want her frightened of Mother. It was easier for her to be brave if she thought Mother was no better than Agnes.

He lay back, and still hadn't let go of her hand. Perhaps he should, but he didn't want to. Instead, he ran his thumb over her knuckles as he had last night, and heard her gasp. He stopped and turned his head her way. "How long will we fish?" Nervous, he let go her hand, turned onto his side and propped his head up with his hand. "I could take a nap."

She smiled. "Why don't you? I often do."

"Really?"

She nodded with a mischievous smile.

"Do you fish here a lot?"

"Daily."

His eyebrows knit. "You must really like fishing."

She swallowed. "I really like eating."

"Fish?"

She nodded as she blushed.

Oliver's smile faded. "You... have to fish in order to eat, is that it?"

She looked at him, cheeks red. "Yes."

He stared at her as something deep inside him snapped. "Etta," he whispered. "How long have you been doing this?"

"Since before Pa died. Difference is, he did a lot of the fishing. But now I have to do it."

He watched her swallow back her embarrassment. "You're surviving the best way you know how. But you won't have to do this any longer."

Her shoulders shook with silent laughter.

"No, really. Apple Blossom is growing and that means more business. You'll see."

"That's just it, Oliver. I can't see. I don't know how."

He pushed himself into a sitting position. "Etta, darling, you won't go hungry, I'll make sure of it."

"But you might leave."

He heard the quaver in her voice, and it almost tore his heart out. He took her by the hand again. "None of us knows what will happen. And even if I do return to England for a time, I'll be back, I promise."

She swallowed again and closed her eyes.

Oliver's own eyes fixed on her lips. The urge to kiss her was overwhelming. But now was not the time.

His eyes widened as she opened hers, and he turned away. Great Scott, did he have feelings toward her? He took a breath. "By Jove, I do."

"Do what?"

He looked at her. "I... well, I have an idea."

"What idea?"

He tried to think but couldn't. He drew closer, his eyes darting to her lips again. "I must speak to my brothers first." Yes, and tell them how you're falling for the blacksmith! Problem was, he wasn't sure she was falling for him. This meant he would have to win her over somehow—no mean feat considering his mother's behavior. If Etta had any sense at all, she'd stay as far away from him as she could get. Being romantically involved with her would only add more problems.

Oliver drew back and sighed. "We should head back."

Etta nodded and retrieved her pole. Silence hung heavy between them now, as if she knew what he was thinking. But how could she? No matter, he needed to concentrate on the real problem, then think about winning the blacksmith.

Chapter Fourteen

Etta stole glances at Oliver on the way back to town. He looked more than a little troubled and she knew why. His mother.

Her chest tightened at the thought. What a horrible woman! But part of her knew Mrs. Darlington was only trying to do what she thought was right. Unfortunately, that didn't align with what was happening in her sons' lives at the moment. They would marry the women they met and fell in love with and that was it. But poor Oliver...

She tried not to grimace at the thought of his mother choosing a bride for him back in England. What sort of woman would she be?

A feeling of unease settled in her stomach as they continued down the trail toward town. She stole another glance at Oliver, who was lost in his thoughts. What else might be going through his mind? Was he worried about his mother's plans for him? Or was he just preoccupied with their recent venture into the woods? Somehow, she doubted the latter, but it would be nice if he thought about it.

She remembered the way his hand had felt in hers as they watched the clouds. She had never felt so alive, so free. But now as they made their way back to town, she couldn't help the nagging feeling that their moment of freedom was ending.

Etta's intuition proved accurate as they returned to town. Oliver's mother was waiting for them at the hotel entrance wearing a stern expression that put Etta on edge. Mrs. Darlington was a force to be reckoned with, and it seemed she always had a plan in mind.

"Oliver, dear," Mrs. Darlington said icily, "I trust your excursion went well?"

"Yes, Mother," Oliver replied, his tone polite but guarded.

"I hope you didn't cause any trouble, young lady," Mrs. Darlington said, turning her attention to Etta. "I trust my son wasn't too much of a burden?"

Etta bristled at the condescending tone, but she answered politely. "No trouble at all, Mrs. Darlington. Oliver was a perfect gentleman."

Mrs. Darlington raised an eyebrow but said nothing for a moment. "Well, I'm glad to hear it. Now, Oliver, we need to discuss your future."

Etta watched Oliver's expression shift from guarded to tense. She knew what was coming next. Mrs.

Darlington *did* have someone in mind for Oliver to marry. Was it someone he'd never met before?

"I've arranged a meeting with the Finchbottoms when we return to England," Mrs. Darlington continued. "Laurel's a lovely young woman and comes from a good family."

Oliver's jaw tightened, but he kept his voice level. "Mother, I've told you before that I have no intention of marrying her."

Etta's heart sank and she tried not to panic. It was bad enough Oliver might return to England and never come back, but to be saddled with a bride he didn't want... why, that would be horrible.

She eyed Oliver's mother. What if was she a powerful woman in England with connections that stretched far beyond her country's borders? If so, and Mrs. Darlington set her sights on finding a suitable wife for her son, there might be little he could do to stop her. Unless he stayed. But she'd heard enough snippets of conversation over the last few days to also know that Oliver and his brothers were dutiful sons who wanted to take care of their parents and the family farm as they aged. They, too, were trying to do the right thing.

She tried to push the thoughts from her mind and focus on the present. Oliver and his mother were staring each other down, the latter wearing a sour expression. Both looked ready to blow.

"Ah, there you are, Mrs. Darlington."

Everyone jumped as Agnes approached. She was

dressed in her Sunday best, and was actually smiling! Etta stared at her and cringed. Agnes had no idea what she was dealing with.

Mrs. Darlington looked her up and down. "And who are you?"

Agnes' smile broadened as she shoved past Etta to stand before the woman. "I'm Agnes Featherstone. I sent the telegram informing you of your sons'..." She glanced at Oliver. "... indiscretions."

Now Mrs. Darlington smiled! Etta fought the urge to take a step back. Oliver didn't hesitate. But in his case, maybe it was to keep from grabbing Agnes by the shoulders, turning her around and sending her back to the bank. "Agnes," he said, jaw tight. "What you did was deplorable and none of your business."

"He's not wrong, you know," Mrs. Darlington said. "It was, at its core, very bad form. However, I am glad you thought to let us know what was going on, or I may not have arrived in time to stop this."

"What?" Etta couldn't help but ask. She gulped as she already knew the answer.

Mrs. Darlington straightened. "My sons' weddings, of course."

Oliver shook his head and faced his mother. "When will you realize you can do nothing?"

"I can disinherit your brothers for their bad choices."

"Mother," he began, jaw as tight as before. "You'd be making a huge mistake. Is your social standing so important to you that you'd risk losing them altogether? Do you really think you can make them bend to your will? What sort of love is that?" He took a step toward her. "It's not. It's the act of a selfish woman who's more afraid of how this will stain the family name than of losing the love and respect of her sons." He turned to Agnes. "And you! This is all your fault."

"Me?" Agnes said, her hand to her chest. "I did what any other self-respecting citizen would do. Your parents are titled, wealthy—of course you and your brothers are doing the wrong thing! Marrying the likes of Letty Henderson, Cassie Laine and..."

Oliver took a step forward. "Don't, Agnes. Just don't."

She swallowed and backed up a step. "Francis is going to hear about this!"

"You can tell Mr. Featherstone whatever you want," Oliver exclaimed, his voice rising. "But it won't change a thing. I've made my decision and I won't be swayed by your or anyone else's opinions."

Mrs. Darlington opened her mouth to say something, but Oliver cut her off. "No, Mother. This is my life and I'll live it as I see fit."

Etta watched in awe as Oliver stood up to his mother. She had never seen him so passionate about anything before. He was determined to make his own choices and live his own life, even if it meant going against his mother's wishes. Bravo!

Mrs. Darlington looked displeased, but there was a glimmer of pride in her eyes as well. "Very well, Oliver," she said, her tone icy. "But remember, there are consequences to every decision."

Oliver nodded stiffly. "I understand."

Etta's shoulders slumped as relief washed over her. Oliver had won this battle, at least for now. But she still didn't like the mention of consequences.

She pondered saying something to Oliver later when the stage suddenly appeared, heading straight for them. She blinked a few times and wondered how much mail it was bringing.

"Afternoon," Frank said as he came out of the hotel.

Mrs. Darlington and Agnes gave him the same look of disdain. "Are you leaving?" Agnes asked.

He shook his head as the stage pulled up in front of the hotel. "No, ma'am." He pulled his gun and pointed it at them. "But you are."

The stage stopped in a cloud of dust, its door flying open. Jonny and his brother Dale grinned as they too pointed their guns right at them.

"In you go, all of you," Frank sneered. "Make one sound, and I'll kill ya where ya stand."

Oliver glanced at Etta, then the hotel.

"Now," Frank demanded.

Jonny hopped out, grabbed Etta and tossed her inside. She heard Oliver curse just before he climbed into the stagecoach followed by his mother and Agnes. She could only hope and pray that neither of them did or said anything to upset Frank and his gang.

Her worst fear had come to life. Outlaws had returned to Apple Blossom.

Oliver sat, his jaw rigid. Only this time it was because Frank had a gun pointed at him. Jonny, the youngest of Frank's gang, smiled as he kept the revolver in his hand pointed at Etta. Frank had crammed his mother and Agnes next to him and sat on the other side of Etta, his gun pointed at them, a grin on his face. "Keep quiet, all of ya, and no one gets hurt, understand?"

"What do you want with us?" Mother snapped.

"Shut up," Frank ordered.

"Mother," Oliver said evenly. "Do as he says." He looked out the window as the stagecoach turned left and started looping its way through what few houses in town there were, and the apple orchards that grew beyond the clearing behind the general store, and Etta's blacksmith shop and livery stable. The lane returned to the little road that led to the main one heading to Virginia City. Great Scott, what did they want with the four of them?

Oliver glanced at his mother, then looked at Etta. Jonny was staring at her neck and practically salivating. Every protective instinct within him roared to life, and it was all he could do to stay wedged between his mother and the stagecoach wall.

As soon as the stage reached the main road, it pulled

to the side and Frank opened the door. "Nobody move or Jonny'll kill the pretty one."

"No, I won't!" Jonny whined. "What a waste that'd be."

Frank sneered at him. "Ya'll kill her if I say so, got that?" He waited a moment, one leg outside the coach. He wasn't leaving, blast it.

Oliver's eyes flicked to Jonny and back. If he left, and he could overpower Jonny and get his gun...

"I got the rope," Dale said as he approached the stage.

"Good, tie 'em up and tie 'em tight." Frank grabbed Agnes and pulled her out of the stage with him. "Dilbert, tie up this one."

"Don't you touch me you... you ruffian!"

Frank rolled his eyes. "And do us all a favor and gag her too. Same goes for Her Majesty in there." He jabbed a thumb over his shoulder at the stage.

Dale climbed in, tossed some rope at Jonny, then aimed his gun at Oliver. "You, get out here." Oliver did as he was told. If he tried to make a move, Dale might shoot his mother.

As soon as he stepped outside the stage, Frank roughly grabbed him, yanked his hands behind his back and lashed them together.

Well, this was a fine mess they were in. If no one paid attention that the stage had only stopped at the hotel and left, it could be a while before anyone discovered they were missing. Father would nap about now, and Mother usually read quietly while he was doing so. Their abductors would have a two-hour head start if that were the case. "What do you want?"

"Money, what else?" Frank yanked on his bonds, making Oliver wince.

"Why didn't you just rob the bank?"

Frank laughed. "From the looks of that place, there ain't much money in the bank. Besides, we got the banker's wife. If there's any decent amount, her husband'll give it to us for her ransom." He looked at the wagon. "Then there's your ma. Now she's worth a pretty penny."

"How dare you abduct us!" Mother spat. "I'll see you hang for this, you worthless worm!"

Frank spun Oliver around. "Gag her too." He stuffed a handkerchief into Oliver's mouth, then tied another over it, effectively gagging him. He then shoved him toward the stagecoach door and forced him back inside. Once seated, Jonny bound his ankles.

Trussed up, gagged and helpless. Crumbs! How was he going to get them all out of this?

He looked at Etta, bound and gagged as he was. She was frightened, he could see it in her eyes, and there was nothing he could do but offer her a reassuring look that said, *I'll get us out of this if I have to die trying*. Problem was, he might. Even Agnes, now being hauled back into the stagecoach by Jonny, looked terrified. The only one that didn't was Mother, who was giving Frank and his gang the same icy stare she'd been giving him before they were abducted.

Dilbert was tying her up and trying not to look her in the eyes. Too bad they only joked about Mother's ability to turn someone to stone with a look. If only it were true, they'd be saved. But that wasn't the case, and though Oliver knew she was trying to intimidate the outlaws, she had to be frightened as well.

As soon as all four of them were bound and gagged, Frank mounted his horse and left Dilbert to guard them. Jonny mounted his own horse and led the horse of whoever was driving the stage. Herbert, perhaps. Oliver couldn't remember if that was right or not. He only knew that if someone didn't realize they were missing and soon, that this could be bad. Very, bad. And there was nothing he could do about it.

Sterling, Conrad and Irving left Mr. Atkins' sawmill and headed back to town. "It was generous of Mr. Atkins to donate logs and lumber for Etta's house," Sterling said.

"Yes, and if we're lucky, Alma or Mr. Hawthorne will donate some of the other things we need," Conrad said. "Nails would be nice."

"One would think Hawthorne would, seeing as how we helped him with his hardware store these last few weeks,' Irving added. "I wonder if Mother has harassed him yet."

"Mother wouldn't be caught dead in a hardware store," Conrad said.

Sterling sighed. "Have either of you spoken to her today?"

"After the disdainful looks she was giving us last night?" Conrad shuddered. "No."

Irving shook his head. "I'm afraid I said nothing other than wish her a good morning when I arrived at the hotel. Father was unusually quiet too, did you notice?"

"I did," Sterling said. "I believe he's tired of this and wants to return home. Unfortunately, we need to come to some sort of agreement with him and leave Mother out of it. He's let her do things he shouldn't have and now she's lost all reason."

"Phileas gave Father a tour of the hotel today," Irving stated. "He was impressed with what Phileas had done, though I doubt he'll tell Mother."

The three exchanged a look of annoyance. "Perhaps Mother should go home and leave Father with us," Conrad quipped.

Sterling rolled his eyes. "That won't solve anything. Mother will have to accept the fact we're marrying Letty, Cassie, Sarah, Dora and Jean."

"And if she talks Father into disinheriting the lot of us?" Conrad asked.

"If she does, it's because he couldn't take her badgering anymore." Sterling looked down the road and sighed again. "She's having a tantrum. She's no better than a child." He nodded to himself. "She'll get over it. In time."

"You hope." Conrad waved at a fly that was buzzing around his head. "If she keeps up this behavior of hers, our women won't want to marry us."

"They're smart enough not to let Mother get to them," Sterling said. "Letty told me last night she feels sorry for her. I do too."

"The old girl isn't what she used to be," Conrad agreed. "But what's to be done about it?"

"Perhaps we could let Mother spend some time with Sarah and the others," Irving suggested. "She doesn't even know them."

"So long as it's in a controlled setting," Conrad tacked on.

"Of course," Irving agreed.

Sterling adjusted his hat. This entire business with their parents had Letty and the other women upset. "We should talk to the captain when we get back to town and find out if he plans on going to Virginia City soon. If he still hasn't got an answer to his advertisement, then I'll have him speak to a preacher there and make arrangements for our wedding."

Conrad clapped. "Bravo, brother. We may even invite Mother to the wedding."

"Don't jest," Irving scolded. "We will invite her. Father too, of course. And whatever happens, we'll deal with in the proper manner."

Conrad arched an eyebrow at him. "You mean cry and whine over being disinherited?"

"No," Sterling said. "Move on no matter what Mother does and stick to our original plan. Once Mother realizes that we're all she has, she'll see reason. Besides, what woman can resist a grandchild? Letty and I plan on having at least four children."

Irving smiled. "I wouldn't mind a couple more."

Conrad counted on his fingers. "I say, how many mouths do you think I can feed on a deputy's wage?"

Sterling and Irving laughed as they continued toward town. It was getting late and all three were more than a little hungry. Sterling's stomach growled and he put a hand over it as he saw a rider approaching. "Is that Phileas?" Conrad asked.

Sterling peered at their brother's unusually fast approach. "It is..."

"He's moving quickly," Irving observed. He looked at the others. "Something must have happened."

The three exchanged another look before they kicked their horses into a canter and went to meet Phileas.

Chapter Fifteen

Etta was jostled back and forth as their abductors took the stage down a trail that led away from the main road. She saw one of them ride by, heading back the way they came. Probably to hide any evidence that the stage came this way. It was early evening, and she had no idea where they were or what would happen now. She and the rest were still bound, gagged and helpless.

Well, Oliver looked angrier than anything else and his mother... she looked ready to skin Frank and his gang alive. Every time one of them rode by, she stared daggers at them. Not that they paid any attention or cared, but the fact she could keep her icy persona amazed Etta. She wished she could be more like that. Instead, she was scared out of her wits.

She had no idea why they took them other than to ransom Mrs. Darlington. Was it a simple case of being in the wrong place at the wrong time? Maybe it was easier to take all four than to wait until Oliver's mother was by herself. And they didn't want any of them to sound the alarm.

She fought against tears. She hated being this helpless and just wanted to go home. But that wasn't going to happen. For all she knew, they were all going to die at the hands of some half-wit outlaws and for what? Some cash? It was Apple Blossom's worst nightmare come to life and she, Oliver and the others were in the middle of it.

She looked at Oliver, caught the concern in his eyes and tried to smile through the gag, if only to reassure him.

He nodded, then glanced at Agnes and his mother. Agnes was staring at the stagecoach floor while Mrs. Darlington was staring daggers at Dilbert, who'd switched with Dale over two hours ago. If her guess was right, they were heading toward Virginia City, and were getting off the road for the night. They'd left too late in the day to make it to Virginia City by nightfall, so they would have to camp somewhere. She wondered if they would untie them long enough to eat, drink and take care of personal business.

But she could be wrong. They might keep them trussed up like this all night.

When they finally stopped, she slumped against the door in relief and prayed they untied their ankles and let them out. She was cramped, sore and had a horrible headache. She could only imagine how the others were feeling.

Jonny opened the door next her and grinned. "There you are, darlin'. C'mon, let's get you out of there." He yanked her toward him, pulled her out and onto his shoulder, carting her off like a sack of meal. She screamed into the gag in protest but it was no use. He ignored her and headed into the woods.

Uh-oh, this might not bode well for her.

Jonny carried her through some trees and into a campsite. One of them must have ridden ahead to make one while the stage made its way here.

Her captor unceremoniously let her slide off his shoulder and onto the dusty ground. "There. Now don't go nowhere." He grinned at Dale, then headed back the way they came, presumably to fetch another captive.

Dale poked at the ground with a stick and eyed her. "If you promise to be good, I'll untie you for a spell. Make one sound, though, and..." He patted the gun at his hip.

She nodded in understanding. She had to be rid of these bonds!

He took off the gag then untied her, only to tie one end of a long rope to her wrist. "What are you doing?"

"I'm guessing you want to take care of some business?"

Okay, she did. "Fine."

He pulled her into the woods, and they went some distance from the camp. "Well, go on, get it over with."

She went behind a tree and did, and tried to get the rope off her wrist, but it was tied too tight. Drat! Maybe Oliver would have better luck if they did the same routine with the others. Dale had at least fifteen feet of rope, so she had her privacy. If Oliver could somehow use the rope as a weapon...

"C'mon, I ain't got all day," Dale groused.

Drat, drat, drat! "Fine, fine." She emerged from behind some the tree and smoothed her skirt. "Now what?"

"We go back to camp and if you behave, you can have some food and water. If not, then you stay tied up all night, got it?"

"And the others?"

"Same rule applies."

She sighed. At least it wasn't Jonny that brought her deep into the woods. He still had that look in his eye, the one that made her belly go cold. Dale took her arm and took her back to camp. She wondered if they'd untied Mrs. Darlington yet. More to the point, she wondered which one had gotten up the nerve.

She got her answer once they entered the camp and found Agnes and Oliver's mother, their wrists joined by a length of rope. Frank was tying another rope to it so they could be led around. Etta was quick to notice that no one had removed their gags. Cowards.

Dale led them off in the same direction he'd taken her. Now Frank held the end of her tether and was busy tying it to a nearby tree. Etta scanned the small clearing where they'd made their camp. There was no sign of Oliver. Had one of the other men taken him into the woods too?

"Can ya cook?"

She jumped. "What?"

"Cook," Frank said. "I'm hungry. Can ya cook?"

She nodded. "Yes, and I will just as soon as you start a fire." Idiots. A fire would make it easier for a posse to find them. The sooner they got one going, the better.

He smiled at her. "Hmmm, I ain't ever seen a captive so willin' to cook before. Are ya sure ya can? Or is yer cookin' gonna poison us?"

She smiled weakly. "I guess we'll find out."

Frank eyed her before he pulled out a pocket watch and checked the time. "I'd say we have a few hours' head start. Could be wrong, though." He stuck his watch back into his pocket. "Have a seat for now."

She unconsciously rubbed her backside with her free hand. "I'd rather not, if you don't mind."

"Suit yerself." He went to his horse, which had been tethered with the others to a rope strung between two trees, and began to unsaddle it.

Etta looked around for a possible escape route but the woods they were in were too thick. She'd get lost, and so would the others.

How did they get into such a predicament? She wanted to blame Mrs. Darlington. If she hadn't been arguing with Oliver outside the hotel, this might never have happened. But what of Agnes? If she hadn't come along, she and Oliver might not have been waylaid in front of the hotel.

But really, the four of them, whether or not they were arguing, were sitting out in the open, making them easy prey. Now they were stuck in an outlaw camp with a man named Frank who had several idiot outlaws in his gang. The best thing she or the others could do was target the less mindful of the bunch and trick them into helping them escape. No mean feat, as even an imbecile had eyes occasionally. She just hoped this wasn't one of them.

Oliver came stumbling out of the woods as Dilbert shoved him into the campsite. Etta noticed his hands were bound in front of him, and that they'd removed the gag. She hoped they did the same for Agnes and Mrs. Darlington but were probably waiting to have Oliver there for leverage. Threats to his person might keep his mother quiet, but it would do nothing for Agnes. Unless she realized the full scope of their predicament. One that didn't look good.

Oliver was suddenly at her side. "Are you quite all right?"

The concern in his voice sent warmth into her bones. "Yes." She glanced at the outlaws busying themselves around the camp. "And you?"

"Fine." He looked around too. "They don't want to kill us. Rather, they want money. Especially for Mother and me."

"Does your family have any?"

He looked into her eyes. "Some."

She leaned toward him. "Are your parents in the habit of carrying a lot of money with them when they travel?"

"Occasionally. Suffice to say, Father will do what he can." He drew closer. "I'm more interested in what Cassie will do about now. Will she round up a posse and come after us?"

"I'm sure she will. The question is, when? I have no idea how long it took people to realize we went missing."

"Right." Oliver looked into her eyes. "Don't be afraid, Etta. I'll protect you."

"And the others?"

"Of course." He half-smiled. "But I'm not protecting our abductors from my mother."

"Phileas," Sterling shouted before he reached him. "What is it, what's wrong?"

"It's Mother! She's missing!" he shouted back. Both reined their horses to a skidding stop when they reached each other. "And so is Oliver."

"What?" Conrad said as he joined them.

Irving was right behind him. "Great Scott, what happened?"

Phileas' closed his eyes a moment. "Exactly what our women feared. Outlaws. Only instead of robbing the bank, they abducted Mother, Oliver, Etta and..." He opened his eyes. "Agnes."

"Agnes!" Conrad looked at the others. "This is a terrible thing to say, all things considered, but who do we feel sorrier for? Our friends and family, or the outlaws?"

Sterling sighed. "Both. Mother's likely to drive them so crazy one of them shoots her."

"And what about Agnes?" Irving asked. "I know she can't hold a candle to Mother, but she makes a splendid effort."

"They won't shoot them," Phileas said. "Not if they want a ransom. Agnes, Mother and Oliver are worth money. But Etta..."

"Lord help her," Sterling said. "Conrad, get back to town, help Cassie form a posse."

Conrad nodded and was off like a shot.

"Cassie and the captain have already started gathering one," Phileas told the others. "Several people saw the stage come through, but it wasn't until Alma noticed they didn't drop off the mail that she went to find me. And that's only because Billy was looking for bugs on the other side of the library and said he saw the stage pick up passengers in front of the hotel."

"When was all this? We've been helping Mr. Atkins with some things." Sterling glanced at Irving. "We've been gone for at least three hours."

"They have at least that much of a lead," Phileas said. "Alma was upstairs having her lunch when the stage came. The driver just puts the mail at the end of the counter in a basket she has there, then takes any outgoing mail. Folks check the basket as they come into the store."

"But didn't she notice that no mail had been brought inside?" Irving asked.

"No," Phileas said. "Because the outgoing mail never left the basket. Alma saw mail in the basket and didn't realize it was still the outgoing post."

"And Father?" Sterling asked as they started back to town.

"He was napping, then read a book," Phileas said as their horses broke into a gallop. "He's not going to look a gift horse in the mouth. Any time away from Mother is nice."

Sterling couldn't argue with him there. Mother had probably been nagging poor Father's ear off.

When they reached town, Captain Stanley was saddling his horse in front of the saloon. Mr. McSweeney was next to him, saddling his own. Both looked grave, and Sterling tried not to panic. He dismounted his horse and joined them. "Where are the women?"

Captain Stanley smiled. "You need not worry about your future brides. All are safe."

Sterling breathed a sigh of relief. "Thank goodness for that. Who's the best tracker in town?"

"That would be me," Mr. McSweeney said. "I learned to track when I learned how to find wild mushrooms, roots and berries."

Irving blinked a few times. "I'm not going to ask."

"Suffice to say, McSweeney is all we've got," Phileas

chimed in. "And I, for one, will take him. Time is of the essence, and I think we all know why."

The captain frowned. "Etta."

Mr. Featherstone came running down the street. "Thank Heaven you're here! Sterling, you've got to do something! My poor Agnes!"

He nodded and patted Mr. Featherstone on the shoulder. "Don't worry, we'll find her."

Captain Stanley took his other shoulder. "Francis, you stay behind in case Agnes or one of the others manages to escape and make their way back here. I think I have a good idea where these fellows might be headed. And they won't make it there today. They'll have to camp somewhere."

"And that's how we'll catch up to them," Sterling said.

"Aye."

"Where's Father?" Irving asked.

"Inside—follow me." Phileas led them into the hotel to find their father sitting at the large dining table, a plate of untouched food in front of him. Sterling knew their father liked to snack when he was nervous, but he had eaten nothing.

"Sterling, there you are. You've heard?"

"Yes." He pulled out the chair next to him and sat. "We'll find them."

"Quickly, I hope. Your mother doesn't know when to hold her tongue and you know what might happen."

"I do."

Father looked him in the eyes. "I know she's a nag and always has to have her way and, dash it all, I've allowed it to go on for far too long. This is all my fault."

"You had nothing to do with her being taken. Has anyone found a ransom note?"

"Not yet." He picked up his fork, then set it back down. "I can't even eat, I'm so upset."

"Of course you are, Father," Sterling put a hand over his. "We all are, but rest assured, we'll find them and bring them home."

His father stared at his plate a moment, then looked at him. "Which home?"

Sterling sighed. "Apple Blossom, Father."

He looked around the dining room. "I suppose this is your home now." He smiled at Sterling. "Live here with my blessing."

"Father." Phileas took a seat. "Do you mean that?"

"I do. Your mother will have to get used to it. I'll not disinherit any of you just because you fell in love. Dora has been so kind since we discovered your mother went missing." He stared at his plate again.

"You needn't worry about a thing, Father." Sterling gave his hand a squeeze. "We'll set this to rights and get everything sorted. We have a plan, a good one, but now is not the time to tell you."

He nodded. "I look forward to hearing it. But first, bring your mother and my boy back to me."

Sterling nodded. "We will." He left the chair and

motioned to the rest to follow him. He went outside and headed back to the saloon and their horses.

Conrad was there with Cassie and he knew what was coming. His brother was eyeing his betrothed, a determined look on his face. "I won't have it," Conrad said. "You are not going."

Cassie's hands went to her hips. "I'm the sheriff, Conrad—of course I am. Besides which, I'm your boss. I'm the one that can order you what to do, not the other way around."

Sterling tried to hide a smile.

Phileas didn't. "This is no time to have a lover's spat. Lives are at stake! Besides which, she can shoot better than you, Conrad."

Conrad sighed. They all knew it was true. "Very well, but you're to stay out of the line of fire."

Cassie laughed. "I'll be the one firing, sweetheart." She kissed him on the cheek, then adjusted the saddlebags on her horse.

Wallis hurried across the street from Alma's. "I've got more ammunition." He went to his horse and put the box of bullets in his saddlebags. "Are we ready?"

Before anyone could answer, Mr. Featherstone came running toward them waving a piece of paper. "I found it!"

"What the devil?" Sterling muttered.

Wallis glanced his way. "Once we figured out Mother was missing along with Jean's hotel guests, we also figured they had to have left some sort of ransom note."

Mr. Featherstone reached them huffing and puffing. "Here." He held it up to no one in particular.

Sterling took it and read it aloud. "To the fancy English fella, we got your wife. To the banker. We got yours too. Bring $10,000 to the fork in the road leading to Virginia City by noon tomorrow and we won't kill them."

"Noon!" Mr. Featherstone blanched. "We don't have that much money in the bank." He facepalmed then let his hand slid down to his chin. "Come to think of it, we don't have any money." He turned to the captain. "Quick, fetch it!"

The captain made a face and arched one bushy eyebrow. "I can't."

"What?" Irving said. "Why not?"

"I don't know where it is."

"WHAT?!" everyone cried.

Sterling gaped at him. "Captain, what have you done?"

He shrugged. "Well, in case them fellas turned out to be outlaws, I didn't want them figuring out we hid the money, see. So after Francis had me bury it, I had some of my crew dig it up and bury it too. That way if I was tortured to disclose its location, I couldn't tell them."

Everyone's jaw dropped simultaneously.

"That's a right good idea," Mr. McSweeney said.

Sterling counted to ten, then asked, "Who dug it up and reburied it?"

"Well... if I told you, then I'd be putting that crew

member in danger. And besides, I have no idea which one buried it."

Phileas turned to his horse and let his head fall against the saddle. "Mother and Oliver are doomed."

"Now it's not as bad as all that," Captain Stanley said. "I'll ask the crew myself."

Conrad exchanged a look with Cassie. "Billy?"

Captain Stanley smiled. "Aye. He's a good lad and so I put him in charge. Wouldn't be the first time my crew has buried some treasure."

Sterling sighed. "Right, then. Who's going to speak to Billy?"

"I will, of course," the captain said.

Phileas came away from his horse. "I'll go with you."

Sterling watched them set off. "While they're looking for the bank's money, the rest of us can look for Mother, Oliver, Agnes and Etta. With any luck, we'll find and rescue them before there's any need for the ransom to be paid."

Chapter Sixteen

Etta watched warily at the outlaws built a quick fire and tried not to shake her head at them. What a bunch of idiots! She hoped Oliver's brothers and whomever else Cassie could round up for a posse were already looking for them. With any luck, they'd smell the smoke from the road and find them that way.

Frank and Dilbert were to head for Virginia City. From what snippets of conversation she'd been able to decipher, they planned on robbing the bank there while the rest collected the ransom. Then they would meet up and make a run for it. The only snafu she could detect in the plan was that there was no mention of releasing them. Would they simply collect the loot and, after trussing her and the rest up somewhere, tell Oliver's brothers the location? Good grief, they weren't planning on killing them, were they? That's not how it worked!

She gulped at the thought as Jonny worked to open several cans of beans.

"Etta," Oliver whispered to her.

She looked his way. "Yes?"

"Can you loosen the rope on your wrist at all?"

"No," she whispered back. "I've tried but it's no use. It's cutting my circulation off as it is."

"Dash it all," he hissed. His hands were bound before him, and they'd tied him and the others to the same tree. After giving Agnes and Oliver's mother some water, they'd re-gagged them. None of Frank's gang were going to take any chances of getting a tongue lashing from either woman. The temptation to shoot them would probably be too much. One more reason to relax a little, she thought.

Etta inclined her ear toward Agnes, who softly snored. She doubted Mrs. Darlington was snoozing. She was probably chewing her way through the gag and would let loose on the outlaws with a vengeance once she did.

"Can you loosen my bonds?" Oliver whispered.

She looked at him. Why hadn't she thought of that? They were close enough to each other. "I can try." She scooted a little closer. Jonny was banging a can of beans against the edge of a cook pot to get the contents into it.

"Careful now," Oliver whispered. "Don't let him see you."

"This could take a while. He wants me to mind the pot."

"That's fine," Oliver whispered back. "But whenever you can, come to me and fiddle with these ropes. Over time we'll get them off."

She nodded at him just as Jonny reached for another can. "Get over here, will ya? I ain't tending these beans."

She got to her feet. The length of rope barely reached the fire, but she'd manage. "Can't you take Agnes' and Mrs. Darlington's gags off?"

"What? And have to listen to them two bellyache all night?"

"I'm sure that if they promise not to, they'll be quiet." She looked at Agnes. She must have heard her name – she was looking right at them. Mrs. Darlington, who was bound on the other side of the tree, was probably calculating what to do.

Etta sighed. "They'll need water again."

Jonny rolled his eyes. "You are the fussiest captives I've ever seen."

She looked at him. "You've had others?"

"No, you're the first. But I still think you're all fussy."

She stood straight. "Never underestimate the power of a good deed."

His face screwed up in confusion. "Huh?"

Etta could see that Jonny wasn't the smartest of the bunch. "Show kindness to someone and they'll show kindness to you."

He glanced at the tree where the others were tied.

"Does that mean they won't talk my ear off and call me all them fancy swear names?"

Etta tried not to smile. "Those were not swear words Mrs. Darlington was using earlier." Okay, so she didn't recognize many of them either, but they didn't sound like swearing. Besides, Mrs. Darlington was too much of a lady to swear. "Please?"

Jonny smiled. "Tell ya what, I'll take off their gags if *you* give me a little kiss."

She gasped. As did Oliver. "What?" he said. "Out of the question!"

"You stay out of this," Jonny spat.

Etta took a deep breath. "Fine, just take off their gags."

Jonny grinned ear to ear, eyes bright, then pursed his lips together and closed his eyes.

Etta grimaced as Oliver shook his head and mouthed the word no.

She gave him a helpless shrug, then leaned toward Jonny. Thankfully, the rope wasn't letting her get near him so she did the next best thing. She kissed the tips of two fingers, reached out and tapped them on his lips.

His eyes sprang open. "Hey, what was that?" His face screwed up again. "That wasn't no kiss."

"It was the best I could do under the circumstances."

"What circumstances?"

She backed up a couple of steps then raised her wrist with the rope tied around it. "You were too far away."

Jonny looked at his feet. "Well, doggone." He took several steps toward her. "Now kiss me."

"No. A bargain is a bargain, and I gave you a kiss already."

Jonny gaped at her, then looked at Oliver. "Is this how she kisses you?"

Oliver's eyebrows shot up. "Well, no. I've never kissed her."

Jonny rolled his eyes in annoyance. "You know what I mean."

Oliver shrugged. "I'm afraid I don't."

Jonny looked at him in shock. "You mean to tell me you've never kissed her?"

He shrugged again. "Never."

"Huh," Jonny scoffed. "You're lying."

Oliver looked Etta in the eyes. "I wish I was."

Her chest warmed at his words as part of her melted. He wanted to kiss her?

Jonny reached for Etta as Dale and Herbert returned with several of the horses they'd taken to a nearby creek to water. "What are you doing?" Herbert barked. "The beans are burning!"

Jonny snatched a spoon off a rock and handed it to Etta. "Don't just stand there, stir 'em!"

She rolled her eyes and did, then dumped the other two cans into the pot. "You're fire is too hot for cooking."

"Don't matter," Dilbert said. "The beans'll cook faster."

Herbert watched as Jonny headed for Agnes and Mrs. Darlington. "What do you think you're doing?"

Jonny stopped in front of Agnes. "They need water."

"Who says?"

He pointed at Etta.

She fought the urge to roll her eyes again. "It's been hours," she argued.

Herbert cringed. "Ain't been long enough as far as I'm concerned. "

"They'll keep quiet," she argued, and hoped it was true. If not, one of them, mostly likely Agnes, would get shot. Mrs. Darlington was worth more.

"Fine, but just for a little while," Herbert said. "And only if they stay quiet."

Jonny stood in front of Agnes. "You sure about this?"

Herbert sighed. "Not really, but do it anyway. We wouldn't want to lose our chance at a hefty ransom."

Jonny shrugged and bent to Agnes.

Etta stirred the pot and prayed she held her tongue. Then again, Agnes would probably do whatever Mrs. Darlington did.

Once Jonny removed her gag, he unbound her hands and gave her a canteen to drink from while he went to see to Mrs. Darlington. Agnes, thank goodness, didn't say a word.

Mrs. Darlington coughed and sputtered a few times before Jonny grabbed the canteen from Agnes and handed it to her. "Thank you," she rasped. At least she was being polite.

Oliver tried to see around the tree but couldn't. "I say, have you had enough, Mother?"

"Yes, Oliver, thank you."

Etta gave the beans one last stir then left the pot. If Herbert got mad, so be it, but she had to check on them. "Mrs. Darlington?"

"What is it?"

Etta made her way around the tree to stand before her. Oliver's mother looked tired, but other than that she was fine. She also still looked angry, but was smart enough at this point to know that if she didn't stay quiet, the gag would come back. "Are you hungry?"

She nodded. "Yes. Serve me when the food is ready."

Etta nodded, then went to stand before Agnes. "Are you hungry?"

"What do you think?"

Etta held a finger to her lips, signaling her to be quiet. Agnes sighed. "Yes, dear, I am."

"I'll bring you some beans as soon as they're heated." She left, sending up a prayer of thanks that both women were behaving. There were a few moments that day when she thought one or both would get themselves shot.

Etta returned to the fire, stirred the pot again and tasted the beans. These were the same kind she purchased from Alma's store—at least the outlaws had the foresight to get some supplies before they left town. Whether they planned on having this many mouths to feed, she couldn't say, but at least she and the others hadn't really been harmed. Now all she had to do was pray things stayed that way. "C'mon, Cassie, find us. Before it's too late."

Oliver shouldn't have said what he did about kissing Etta, but the words slipped out before he could stop them. Maybe because part of him feared he'd never get a chance to kiss her. The realization that he wanted to came as no surprise. He liked Etta, even if she was a little skittish. He didn't even mind that she was the town blacksmith at this point. Yes, she smelled like horse half the time and her face was dirty, her clothes careworn, but she was honest, hardworking, and kind.

Laurel Finchbottom was as decent sort, but her brothers weren't. Of the two young ladies, Etta was the better choice. Maybe after they got out of this Mother would agree with him. For now, he had to concentrate on getting them free. No small task as everyone was tied to the same tree and easy to watch. Only Etta could roam somewhat freely, and it might be only a matter of time before they tied her to their tree. He would have to work fast.

Etta knew it too. She came to him with the canteen and placed it in his bound hands. "Here, drink some of this."

His eyes met hers as he raised the canteen to his lips

and drank. She was more beautiful in that moment than he could've imagined. What was he thinking, going back to England and letting Mother choose a wife for him? Had he gone mad? There was a perfectly good choice standing in front of him. Besides, did he really want to be parted from all his brothers for long periods of time? Wouldn't it be easier if they all lived in Apple Blossom and rotated their time in England?

His eyes were still on hers when he handed the canteen back. Etta's blue eyes locked with his as if she was seeing him for the first time. Did she think he was handsome? Was she attracted to him? He wanted to find out, but now was not the time. He couldn't use his earlier faux pas with the kiss to gage anything. She looked as shocked to hear it escape his lips as he was.

"Thank you," he finally said. He nodded toward his left. "My mother?"

"She looks fine."

He breathed a sigh of relief. "Agnes?"

"I'm fine too," she said before Etta could answer. "Thank you for asking."

He smiled. "Glad to hear it." He closed his eyes a moment, trying to think. The only plan he'd come up with so far was to have Etta try to loosen his bonds when she could. It wasn't the best plan, but it was all he had at the moment.

Etta served the outlaws their beans, then prepared plates for the rest of them. Dilbert untied their hands so they could eat and Etta must have had a thought as her eyes flashed just before she looked at him. Oliver caught the tiniest hint of a smile, then it was gone. Good. Maybe she was planning on slipping him a knife.

"I should take Agnes and Mrs. Darlington to the creek to wash up," Etta suggested.

"Wash up?" Herbert scoffed. "This ain't no fancy hotel, missy."

"You've never been in a fancy hotel," Mrs. Darlington commented from her side of the tree. "How would you know?"

Herbert left the rock he was sitting on. "How do you know if I haven't?"

"I can tell."

"So can I," Agnes added.

Oliver thought he heard Mother scoff, but wasn't sure. "Be polite," he mouthed.

"But Etta is right," Mother said. "I wouldn't mind washing up."

Herbert sighed in disgust. "Fine. I suppose it's better to do it now than have to listen to you bellyache half the night about it. Jonny!"

"What, me? Why do I have to take 'em?"

"We both will. Dilbert can stay and watch over that one." He nodded at Oliver.

"Oh, all right." Jonny wolfed down what was left on his plate, walked to the fire and set it down by Etta. "Wash that."

"I was planning on taking the dishes to the creek," she said.

Herbert sighed again, but not as dramatically. "Fine, at least the dishes will get cleaned."

"Hey, I'm a good dishwasher," Jonny said.

"No, you're not," Herbert tossed back. "You're the worst dishwasher I've ever seen."

Jonny shrugged, then eyed Etta. "Are you going to wash up in the creek too?"

"Yes," she hedged.

He leered at her. "Me too."

Herbert groaned and threw his empty plate at Jonny. "Don't even think about it. I need you and Dilbert alert and ready in case a posse catches up to us. Understand?"

Jonny's shoulders slumped. "I never get to have any fun." He trudged to the tree and stood in front of Agnes. "All right, you old crow, let's go to the creek."

Etta gathered dishes and tableware, then headed for Oliver to get his. He watched her, hoping against hope she had the same idea he'd had. Sure enough, when she reached him she stumbled, dropping half of her load on top of him.

"For goodness' sake," Mrs. Darlington groused. "Try to be more careful."

"Pick them plates up," Herbert barked.

Etta hurried to comply. "Sorry." She looked at Oliver and wiped some leftover beans off his pants. "I hope that doesn't attract ants." She wiped the beans away with part of her skirt and Oliver felt the knife drop between his legs.

"So do I. Bedding down with an army of ants isn't my idea of a pleasant night."

"Might be fun to watch, though," Jonny laughed.

Etta rolled her eyes as she picked up the plates and tableware, then stood. "Will someone untie me from the tree?"

Herbert went to the tree and got to work undoing the knot. When he was done, he handed his end of the rope to Jonny, who held it in one hand, took hold of Agnes and pulled her to her feet with the other.

Herbert went behind the tree to untie Mother, and Oliver could just imagine the look she was giving the outlaw. At least the outlaw kept his mouth shut. It didn't take much to set her off.

Soon Herbert and Jonny were herding their captives into the trees toward the creek. When they were out of sight, Oliver brushed at his pants where the beans had spilled.

"Don't worry," Dilbert said. "The ants'll clean that right off you."

Oliver smirked at him. "Thanks."

Dilbert chuckled and put some more wood on the fire.

Oliver tried not to smile. With Frank (the only one of the bunch with a brain) gone, he was content to let their captors keep the fire going. The longer they did, the better chance he and the women had of being found by a posse. None of his brothers were that good at tracking, but someone in town had to be.

Speaking of town, would Mr. Featherstone have gathered what money he could to give to the outlaws as ransom? They were asking for more than what the Apple Blossom Bank had in its vault, if his guess was right. Father and Mother could always wire for funds, but that would take time, considering Apple Blossom didn't have a telegraph office. The nearest one was in Virginia City, and he wondered if the outlaws had figured that out yet. As they hadn't mentioned a ransom note, he'd kept his mouth shut. He knew they had to have left one behind, but he wasn't sure of all the particulars.

Oliver reached between his legs for the knife, felt its cold steel, and tried to relax. It wasn't a sharp knife by any means, but would have to do. For all he knew, this was the only chance they'd have to escape, and he'd better not fail. If he did, they might all wind up dead.

Chapter Seventeen

Sterling, Cassie, Conrad, Irving and Mr. McSweeney rode out of town with Mr. Watson, Mr. Miller and Mr. Featherstone, who was hanging onto his saddle horn for dear life. It was obvious the man hadn't ridden in a while, and Sterling hoped he could stay on his horse.

But the banker's lack of riding ability was the least of his worries. He had a sense of unease in the pit of his stomach. They'd gotten a late start as Captain Stanley had to track down Billy and ask where he buried the bank's money. The boy told him, but it had been dug up and buried someplace else by another of the captain's "crew." This meant all the children in town had to be questioned and they couldn't wait anymore.

By the time they left, it was the hottest part of the day and the sun had been beating down on them relentlessly for the last two hours. The dust kicked up by their horses made it difficult to breathe. Conrad was leading the way, followed closely by Cassie, who kept glancing back at Mr. Featherstone worriedly.

In several hours the sun would set, casting long shadows across the dusty road. If they were quick enough, they might see where the outlaws and their captives had got to, and lucky for them, the stagecoach's tracks were only a few hours old.

Mr. McSweeney brought his horse alongside Sterling's. "My guess is they got off the road. They couldn't get to Virginia City before dark, not even considering when they left. They'll have to camp somewhere."

"Yes," Sterling agreed, "but where?"

"They would have driven the stagecoach's horses hard. I bet we'll find signs of them leaving the road soon, so keep a sharp eye out."

Sterling nodded, but couldn't shake the feeling that something was off. It wasn't just that they were chasing after dangerous outlaws who had taken innocent people hostage. No, it was something else entirely. He felt like they were being watched. He scanned the surrounding area carefully, but couldn't see anything out of the ordinary. They rode through a tree dotted landscape that grew thicker with pine the further they traveled. He supposed someone could hide among them, but was it one of the outlaws or someone else? Maybe he was so jumpy, he was imagining things.

But then he glimpsed movement out of the corner of his eye. He twisted his head, but it was gone. Sterling couldn't be sure if it was just a trick of the light or something else entirely. "Did anyone else see that?" he asked, turning to his companions.

They all shook their heads, but Cassie's expression turned serious. "What did you see?"

"I don't know," Sterling replied, his brow furrowing in confusion. "It was something moving in the distance. Probably nothing." But he couldn't shake the feeling that it was something more.

They rode on in silence, each lost in their own thoughts. As the sun dipped below the horizon, Conrad suddenly pulled his horse to a stop. "Tracks," he announced, pointing at the ground.

They all dismounted and gathered around, inspecting the tracks. Sure enough, they were fresh and headed off the road toward a small cluster of rocks in the middle of some brush.

"Looks like they tried to hide that they came this way," Mr. McSweeney said.

"Yes," Irving agreed. "And I don't think they considered that cutting brush to cover said tracks was a bad idea." He pointed to some foliage that had been obviously cut and tossed onto the tracks the stagecoach left behind.

"Great Scott," Conrad cried. "They're imbeciles."

"Lucky for us," Sterling said. "Now let's go. Better keep things quiet."

The trail led them to a small clearing, where they found the remains of a campfire. Conrad crouched and examined the ashes. "It's still warm. They couldn't have left more than an hour ago."

Cassie looked around, studying the area. "They must have moved further into the woods. I'm surprised they were stupid enough to build a fire."

"They won't be as stupid now," Mr. Miller said. "Should we go after them? Or is it too dark to go further?"

"Some of us can go on foot, scan the area and see if they're somewhere nearby," Mr. McSweeney said.

Sterling nodded in agreement. "Mr. McSweeney is right. We need to be smart about this and not rush in blindly if we spot them. We'll split up and search the area. But be careful. These men are dangerous and have hostages."

They divided into two groups, with Sterling leading one and Mr. McSweeney the other. They moved slowly, stealthily. It was getting dark now and soon the only light they'd have would be from the stars above and the rising moon. As they searched, Sterling still couldn't shake the feeling they were being watched. He dismounted and kept glancing over his shoulder but saw nothing out of the ordinary.

Suddenly he heard a rustling in the bushes and raised his gun, ready for anything. But it was just Mr. Featherstone, stumbling through the brush, leading his horse. "What are you doing here, Featherstone?" he hissed.

"I-I wanted to help," the banker stammered. "I can't

just sit around and do nothing while my poor Agnes is in danger."

Sterling sighed and lowered his gun. "Fine. But stay behind me and don't make a sound."

They continued to search, moving deeper into the woods. The only sounds were the crunching of twigs and leaves beneath their feet and the occasional whisper between them. But it wasn't long before they heard something in the distance. A soft rustling of leaves, the snapping of twigs. They froze, listening intently.

And then they saw them. Two figures moving stealthily through the trees, their faces obscured by shadows. They could hear them talking in low voices, but couldn't make out what they were saying.

The others silently joined them and Sterling motioned for Conrad and Irving to follow him as they crept closer. Cassie started after them but Mr. McSweeney and Mr. Miller held her back, regardless of her silent protests.

It was just as well, Sterling could just make out that it was two of the outlaws, carrying rifles. The stood in a tiny meadow, scanning the area, clearly on high alert.

Sterling motioned to his brothers to flank them, and they slowly moved in opposite directions, closing in on the outlaws. When they were within range, Sterling lunged forward and tackled one of them to the ground. Conrad and Irving did the same to the other.

The two outlaws struggled, but it was two against three and the brothers were stronger. They quickly tied the outlaws up and gagged them, then brought them back to the campsite.

The others were waiting for them, guns drawn. Mr. McSweeney was the first to speak. "Well, well, look what the cat dragged in."

"We caught two of them," Conrad told Cassie triumphantly. "The others can't be far behind."

She blew some hair out of her face. "I could have come with you."

"And spoil our fun?" Conrad quipped. "I must say, I'm beginning to like this rescuing business."

"I'm the sheriff, Conrad," she stated.

"This is not the time for a spat." Sterling bent to one outlaw and removed the gag. "Tell me where the others are."

He looked at his counterpart, who could only shrug.

"Tell me," Sterling said sternly. He looked the outlaw over. "Jonny."

Jonny gulped. "Well, ya see, I can tell ya where two of 'em are."

Sterling and the other exchanged a questioning look. "Why only two?"

Jonny glanced at... Dale, was it? "Um, on account two of 'em escaped?"

"Well, that's jolly good," Irving said.

Jonny shook his head. "I don't know about that. I was kinda hoping the two old ladies would have gotten away. Them two scare me."

Mr. Miller snorted, then cleared his throat.

"What?" Mr. Featherstone said. "My Agnes wouldn't hurt a fly."

"Maybe not," Jonny said. "But she and the other one have been torturing us all evening. Problem is, none of us can figure out what the one is saying, so we have to ask. I've never heard so many insults in my life!"

Now Cassie and Conrad snorted. "That's Mother for you," Conrad said.

"So Oliver and Etta escaped," Irving stated.

"Yeah. Lucky dogs," Dale griped.

"That means the outlaws still have the captives they deem worth something," Mr. McSweeney said. "So they're not likely to harm them."

"Unless they keep talking," Jonny said.

"Herbert was gagging them as we were leaving, you idjit," Dale said. "He's not gonna put up with fancy insults."

Sterling sighed in relief. "Where are they?"

"You sure you wanna rescue them two?" Jonny asked. "My ears are still burning!"

"Well," Conrad mused, "as irritating as both of them can be, one is still our mother, and the other is still Mr. Featherstone's wife."

Jonny and Dale gaped at Mr. Featherstone. "You're a much stronger man than we are," Dale said.

Mr. Featherstone shrugged. "I've had years of practice."

Oliver pulled Etta through the trees and underbrush, his face getting slapped more than a few times by low-hanging branches.

His wasn't the only one. "Be careful," Etta said in a harsh whisper. "That last branch almost blinded me."

He stopped, panting. "Terribly sorry." He cupped her face in his hands and tried to assess the damage, but it was too dark. Still, a few scratches on their faces were the least of their worries. They had the outlaws on their tail, and he wasn't sure how many were hunting them. "Come, we have to keep moving. If we can find a good place to hide, you can stay there and I'll go back for Agnes and my mother."

"By yourself? Oliver, you can't."

He squeezed her hand. "I must. I can't protect you and free them at the same time."

"But Oliver..."

What he did next he didn't regret, but at the same time, it wasn't the smartest thing he could have done. He kissed her.

Etta's voice died when his lips touched hers, and he almost forgot they were running for their lives. When he broke the kiss, he looked into her eyes as best he could, considering how dark it was getting. "We must run." He turned as he tightened his grip on her hand and started off again. If they kept going long enough, whoever was chasing them might give up, cut their losses and turn back. Mother and Agnes were, in the eyes of the outlaws, the more valuable assets.

They came to a wall of rock, and Oliver wondered if there were any caves nearby. "Do you know these woods?"

"No," Etta said in a small voice.

He faced her again, and this time pulled her into his arms. "We're going to get out of this, I promise."

"I still can't get over the fact we escaped."

He drew back to look at her. "Thanks to you."

"You're the one that got free."

He fought the urge to kiss her again. "You gave me the knife."

She looked at him, and the urge to kiss her doubled. Did she want to be kissed? He remembered his words from earlier, and wondered if she did too.

"About what I did earlier..."

"I didn't stop talking, I understand..."

"No, Etta, don't think like that. Yes, you were talking but I... oh, dash it all. If not for the circumstances, I'd kiss you again."

She smiled. "So you did want to."

There was no use denying it. "Yes. And I'll kiss you again just as soon as all this is over."

She said nothing, and he thought he caught another smile, but it was getting too dark to tell. He looked up to gauge the height of a wall of rock they'd come to with what moonlight there was. Thankfully, the moon was full and growing brighter by the minute, which also meant they could spy the outlaws coming. But if they weren't careful, they'd be seen by them too.

"If we can get up there, you can see if someone's coming."

"Me?" She grabbed his arm with her other hand. "Where are you going?"

"Back for Agnes and Mother."

"Oh, Oliver, shouldn't we try to make it back to town and get help?"

"I suspect help is on the way, but I have no idea if they've picked up our trail yet."

She nodded in understanding and he noticed she hadn't let go of his arm yet. He wanted to hold her, but didn't dare. Yet... "Etta, would you... I mean..."

"What?" she whispered.

"Allow me to court you when all this is over?"

She stood in silence. "Oliver... I don't think..."

"It was the kiss, wasn't it? You must think me a cad."

"No, I... just don't think..."

"Then I shan't do it again, I promise. Now let's see if we can get up there."

She sighed. "Fine." She looked up. "How?"

He followed her gaze and tried to listen for any sounds of pursuit. There were none. "I don't know, but we need to find a way." He crept along the wall of rock. Once they found the end of it, they might also find a roundabout way to get to the top.

"Oliver," Etta whispered behind him.

He glanced over his shoulder at him. "Yes?"

"Why would you want to court me?"

HIs chest went tight. "Why would a man *not* want to?"

"I can think of one reason. Your mother."

He knew she was going to say that, but had hoped he was wrong. "Let's leave my mother out of this. If not for her, we might not be here."

"She's a proper lady, isn't she?"

He heard what sounded like disappointment in her voice. "Yes, she is, but that doesn't make her a peach. My mother can be cruel, yet also generous, kind, and forthright. She does what she thinks is best and won't hesitate to let a person know when she disapproves of something or someone."

"Like the men that abducted us?"

He cringed. In a matter of minutes, Mother had insulted their captors in every way she knew how without being impolite about it. She was a master wordsmith.

"She doesn't like me," Etta whispered.

"What?" He took her other hand in his. "Nonsense."

"I'm not good enough."

He stared at her. "Etta, we haven't time for this."

"You asked me if you could court me. And I'm telling you no."

Even as dark as it was, he could see the determination in her eyes. "But Etta..."

"No, Oliver. You can't court me." She pulled her hands from his grasp and continued along the rock wall, looking for a way up.

He watched her a moment. There was no time for

discussion. She feared Mother would never approve of her. Especially since he was the only one left for Mother to marry off to someone of her choosing. If he chose Etta, Mother might try to make poor Etta's life miserable. Maybe she was refusing him out of self-preservation.

But he didn't have time to think about that now. He had to get her safely hidden, then go back for the others. If he thought this was going to be a fight to free them, he could only imagine the fight he would have with Mother if he told her he planned to court the blacksmith.

"There." Etta pointed. "I think we can climb up this way."

Oliver joined her, looked up the steep incline that led to the top of the rock wall, and blew out a long breath. "That's some climb, but at least we can use what trees there are to help." He stilled, listened, then began the steep climb up the side of the hill.

Chapter Eighteen

Etta scrambled up the hillside behind Oliver. Her shorter legs made it hard to keep up with him, and he often backtracked to take her hand and help her along. She wished she was taller, stronger. She hated slowing them down, but there wasn't much she could do about it.

"We're almost there," Oliver whispered just above her. "Be careful now. Sound carries."

"All right," she whispered back.

"That's my girl. Now come on." He offered his hand again.

She grabbed it and he pulled her up to the tree branch he'd grabbed onto. They used it to pull themselves higher up the steep hillside. They were almost to the top now.

When they finally reached it, both were breathing hard. But Oliver didn't stop. He took her hand and skirted the top of the small plateau until he came to a small gathering of rocks. "Right, this will do." As before, he took her hands in his and looked into her eyes. "I want you to stay here. If you hear something, you should be able to see anyone coming across that clearing down there. If they start up the hill, then I want you to run."

"But Oliver..."

He held up his hand, and part of her wanted him to kiss her again, but that wasn't going to happen. After he'd had a little time to think about things, he'd realize she was right and his mother would never allow him to court someone like her. She was so far beneath the Darlingtons, it was pathetic. After listening to the outlaws argue with his mother, she concluded the Darlingtons were not only rich, but nobility. They had a title, and even she knew what that meant. She was scum compared to them.

"Etta," he whispered. "You'll be safe here."

She closed her eyes and tried to keep her mouth shut. No, she'd never be safe anymore. Her heart would forever search for his, and he would wind up marrying some noblewoman in England.

"Etta darling, are you all right?"

His voice was so gentle and concerned that she almost melted into a puddle. No one had ever spoken to her like that. She would never be all right again. Oh, why did he have to be so perfect? And why, in such a short amount of time, did she have to become so attracted to him? Was it because he eased her fears while they were still held captive? Or was it the protective look in his eyes as he watched over her in the outlaws' camp? Whatever it was, it was too late.

"I must go," he whispered. "Stay hidden, understand? If you hear something, take a peek, but do not come out from behind these rocks."

She nodded and hoped he didn't notice the tear making its way down her cheek. She'd wipe it away, but didn't want to draw attention to it.

He drew closer. "I'll come back for you. I promise."

Etta closed her eyes as more tears threatened. Maybe it was the trauma of being abducted, bound, gagged, then forced to cook for their captors. Or maybe she was that attracted to Oliver Darlington.

"Etta?"

She forced herself to nod.

"Good girl." He pulled her into his arms for a quick hug, then disappeared into the darkness.

Etta heard him scuttle back along the top of the plateau, then start down the hill. There was no way to be quiet about any of it, as fast as he was going. She just hoped he could do what he had in mind. Would he even make his way back to the outlaws' camp? She hadn't been paying attention to where they were going when they made a run for it, and hoped Oliver had.

She settled herself in the middle of the rocks and hoped there was nothing else in here with her. Rattlers came to mind, and she shivered, drawing her knees up and hugging them.

As she sat, she tried to recall all the things Mrs. Darlington had spewed at their captors. She used words like *gollumpus* and *jolterhead*. *Gundiguts* came out too. Etta had no idea what these words meant but could guess judging from the tone with which Oliver's mother delivered them. She'd called Herbert something that sound like *shabbaroon*, and even Agnes look impressed. Did she know what the word meant? *Tatterdemalion*. Now there was a word.

In fact, there were so many odd words coming out of Oliver's mother at one point that all five outlaws lined up in front of her and stared, bug-eyed at the woman. But when she called Jonny an unlicked cub, they got the gist of that one and realized she was insulting them.

Etta's favorite, however, was when she told Herbert that he was on his way to becoming a *death's head upon a mopstick*. Etta, unable to stand it any longer, asked Mrs. Darlington what it meant as they headed back to a new tree to be bound to. "It means he'll become nothing but a miserable emaciated chap. And all because he'll not have a penny to his name. No good will come of this, you watch."

Jonny laughed at her tirade and then laughed at her. "Insults from a woman don't mean nothing," he said.

Mrs. Darlington narrowed her eyes at him and said, "Mark my words, young man, one day all of you will face a judge, you *corny-faced scrub*!"

Jonny looked taken aback for a moment or two, then slunk off somewhere.

"And what did that mean?" Etta had asked.

Mrs. Darlington smiled. "That he's a pimple-faced, mean fellow that only ever gets hired to do filthy work. The kind no one else likes to do."

Etta eyed Jonny. "Like abduct innocent women?"

"I was thinking more like rat catchers, but I suppose that could be considered."

Etta had kept talking, all the while knowing that Oliver was sawing through his bonds as fast as he could. Once he was done, he would signal her. It was only a matter of time before they would make their escape. Problem was, only the two of them could get away. They'd have to make a run for it, hide, then circle back and break Agnes and Mrs. Darlington from their bonds.

Sitting in the middle of three large rocks as shelter wasn't what Etta had had in mind. What if Oliver was captured again? Then what would she do? They left with no food. They found a stream during their flight and stopped long enough to drink, but had nothing to carry water in. If she'd been smart, she'd have at least gotten her hands on a canteen. But she wasn't thinking. She only wanted to escape as fast as she could.

She thought she heard something and froze. Oh, no!

Slowly she got to her feet and peeked around one rock to scan the clearing below. There was nothing there. Her heart was beating so loud she couldn't hear anything at this point. What if it was the outlaws? Frank and Dilbert had returned to them, neither of them keen on riding to Virginia City in the dark. Frank had to have sent someone after them. Maybe all were hunting them. Agnes and Mrs. Darlington had been re-tied to a tree. It would be easy enough to gag them and give chase. They could then split up and find them quicker that way.

She gulped at the thought and prayed she was wrong. If they had all given chase and split up as she thought, then Oliver ran a good chance of bumping into some of them and being taken again. They might even shoot him! "Oh, no!" she whispered to herself.

She peeked over the rock again and caught sight of two men coming out of the trees into the small meadow below. "Jonny," she whispered when she recognized him. The other looked like his brother Dale. Both had been eyeing her like she was dessert. If they caught her, who knew what they might do with her before dragging her back to their camp?

Etta got on her knees and sent up a silent prayer that both were too lazy to try to climb the hill and get to where she was.

Oliver crept through the underbrush as quietly as he could. He'd made it back to the outlaws' camp and was relieved to find only Frank left to guard their captives, neither of which looked happy. Mother was now tied right next to Agnes and both were gagged. And were they glaring at Frank? It sure looked like it.

"Where is everybody?" Frank groused as he paced in

front of the fire. That he'd made a fire surprised Oliver. He got mad when he discovered Jonny had built one, but the smell of food caught him and he ate beans with the rest of them, had them clean up the camp before it got too dark, then moved them deeper into the woods. The stage couldn't make it this far, so they'd hidden it about a quarter-mile away but brought the horses with them. Would they set out on horseback tomorrow or retrieve the stage?

He'd heard Dilbert or Dale mention something about robbing the bank in Virginia City. Again. Obviously, it was all part of their plan but they weren't doing so well in executing it. Losing their captives didn't help. Oliver smiled at the thought and crept closer. With any luck, Frank would run off to help the others look. And if he was really lucky, his brothers would also look and would spot Frank's fire.

"Stupid idjits!" Frank kicked dirt at the flames. "I never shoulda taken up with those Coolidge brothers and their cousin. They gotta be the dumbest bunch of yahoos I ever met." He turned to the women and pointed at the fire. "You know the only reason I built this is 'cause I know they're too dumb to find their way back here. In fact, I'll wager I'm gonna have to go out there and find 'em myself!" He kicked dirt at the fire again, extinguishing part of it. "I should go rob the bank alone. I'd be better off."

He paced some more, and Oliver prayed that he did just that. Then his job would be easy.

His mother and Agnes were probably hoping the same thing as they were watching him closely. Agnes looked hopeful. Mother still looked like she wanted to tear him limb from limb for subjecting her to such treatment. Frank didn't know it yet, but he'd be much better off if he left the women there, cut his losses and fled.

"That does it!" Frank griped, then reached for a canteen. "You two can stay tied to that tree 'til the coyotes find you. I'm leavin'! This was a bad idea from the start." He tossed water onto the fire as he kicked more dirt onto it, killing the flames.

Agnes squeaked, and Oliver couldn't blame her. There were all manner of wild beasts in the woods, several of which wouldn't mind making a meal out of them.

Oliver ignored the growling sound his mother made and watched Frank quickly gather a few things, then saddled his horse. He cursed a few times about dousing the fire too soon, then got back to work.

Oliver tried not to make a sound as the one outlaw with half a brain continued to mutter to himself and finally mounted his horse.

"About time," Oliver whispered. But he'd wait as long as he had to until Frank left. Unfortunately, he still had to free his mother and Agnes, then get back to Etta. It was pure luck he found his way back here. But he smelled the smoke from the fire and eventually saw it through the trees. If Frank hadn't built one, he could have stumbled right by the camp and not known it unless he heard Frank's little tantrum.

Oliver waited a few minutes after Frank rode off before sneaking into the camp. What if this was a trap and one of the other outlaws was lurking nearby, waiting to shoot at anything that moved? "Mother?" he whispered. He heard a muffled cry and headed for the sound.

The trees were so thick here it was almost impossible to see. "Mother, Agnes, I'm here." He spotted them, and as soon as he reached them, removed their gags, then put a finger to his lips. "Not a sound," he whispered. He untied them as fast as he could. Frank might change his mind and figure it was still easier to ransom them than rob the bank in Virginia City. "Can you stand?"

"We're not helpless," Mother spat. "Come along, Agnes." His mother got to her feet then offered a hand to Agnes.

Oliver watched in fascination. "Etta is hiding a mile or so from here."

Agnes, on her feet now, glanced around. "What if they find her?"

"I doubt they will. Now follow me." He took Agnes' hand, who grabbed one of Mother's, and they were off.

Twigs snapped and clothes tore as the women's skirts caught on brush, but other than that, he heard nothing that sounded like pursuit. At one point he stopped and thought he'd heard something, but there were only the usual night sounds, crickets and the distant yip of a coyote. But it was the sense that something was watching them that had him unnerved, and he tried to hurry the women along as he retraced his steps as best he could through the woods to the clearing he and Etta crossed before reaching the rock wall.

"How much further?" Mother asked.

"Not far now." Oliver stopped. "Do you need to rest?"

"For a moment. My shins are killing me. This horrid underbrush has ruined my dress."

"Better your dress than your life," Agnes said.

"What are you worried about?" Mother said. "That dress of yours is easily replaced. You can make yourself a new one. This is Paris fashion I'm wearing–"

Oliver rolled his eyes. "Ladies, please. Let's not argue."

"She started it," Agnes said.

"And I'll finish it. This was an uncalled-for experience I do not wish to repeat," Mother said. "As soon as we get back to town, I want those men hunted down and brought to justice!"

"Mother, keep your voice down."

"And another thing," she said, ignoring him. "We're returning to England, and you're going with us. At least one of you is still free from the clutches of Apple Blossom. What a joke."

"Now see here," Agnes said. Even in the dark Oliver could see her wagging a finger at his mother. "There is nothing wrong with our little town. We're respectable people, all of us. You just don't think our women are good enough for your sons."

"They're not," Mother shot back. "None of them. And I'll not see Oliver be roped into a relationship he doesn't want."

"As if you aren't planning on doing the same to him?" Agnes said.

Oliver sighed. She had a point. "Can we leave now?"

"You keep out of this!" Mother barked.

"Quiet," Oliver warned.

"I can see now that I never should have sent that telegram," Agnes said.

"I second that," Oliver muttered. At this rate, someone was going to hear them and they'd find themselves tied up all over again.

"Well," Mother said. "I suppose I should thank you for that."

"Indeed, you should.' Agnes harrumphed.

"Please, can we continue on?" Oliver asked.

"Well don't just stand there," Mother said. "Get moving. I don't know why you stopped in the first place." She shoved past him and stumbled ahead.

Oliver sighed as Agnes followed her without a word, then did the same.

Chapter Nineteen

As the moon rose higher over the Montana wilderness, the tired foursome huddled around a patch of damp wood, shivering from the night's growing cold. It had rained about an hour ago. Late summer storms weren't unusual, and Etta, Oliver, Mrs. Darlington and Agnes got soaked.

Etta watched Oliver's look of determination in the moonlight as he knelt down, his long limbs folding gracefully despite their weariness. He knew she and the others were counting on him, and hoped he didn't let them down. After all, what did an Englishman know about surviving in the wilderness?

But he'd come back for her, just as he said he would, and found her hiding halfway down the steep hill they'd climbed to get to the top of the plateau. She saw men in the moonlight and was trying to make her way away from the plateau. Luckily Oliver had found her when he had. She might have gotten lost in the woods, or worse, recaptured by the outlaws.

"Watch closely, Mother," Oliver said, his English accent cutting through the silence like a knife. "You're about to witness an extraordinary feat."

"Starting a fire with wet wood?" she scoffed. "Good luck with that."

Oliver retorted with a grin, his boyish charm evident in the moonlight despite the dire situation. With deft hands, he expertly shaved off the damp outer layer of the wood, revealing the dry core beneath. Next, he lit a match to his carefully laid kindling, and within moments a small flame flickered to life.

"Well, what do you know!" Agnes exclaimed. "How did you manage that?"

"Let's just say I've been paying careful attention to the captain and Mr. McSweeney's adventure stories." he replied, casting a quick glance at Etta. "But enough of that." He stood and looked toward a river that lay about five miles outside of Apple Blossom. They would have to cross it if they continued this way. Etta hoped they didn't. But if the outlaws kept them from finding the road and their way back to town, they might have to.

Etta watched the fire grow and scooted closer to the warmth. She had to admit, she had a sense of pride in the way Oliver rescued them and was now doing his best to protect her and the others. This was not the boy that had arrived in town all those weeks ago with his brothers. And, she had to admit, that's how she'd thought of him at first. But now she saw a man determined to see them to safety. Her heart melted at the thought and her growing feelings for him ignited all over again.

He sat beside her. "How are you holding up?"

She brushed a lock of wet hair off her face. "Thank you for building a fire, but it might draw the attention of Herbert and the others. Maybe even Frank."

"Perhaps," Oliver mused. "But for now, let's focus on getting warm and dry. It wouldn't do for the lot of us to catch our deaths out here."

She nodded her agreement as a twig snapped somewhere in the darkness. "Oliver," she said softly, "I heard something."

"What?" Mrs. Darlington looked around. "Is it those ruffians?"

"Shush, Mother," Oliver commanded. Everyone went silent, the stillness of the night punctuated by the sound of their breathing. In the distance, a low growl echoed through the trees—a menacing, guttural snarl that sent shivers down Etta's spine.

"Sounds like wolves," Agnes whispered, her voice trembling with fear.

"Stay together and stand your ground," Oliver instructed, his tone steady. "We can scare them off if we make ourselves look bigger and louder. That's what the captain says."

"The captain?" Agnes groused. "And you believed him? I doubt he's ever encountered a wolf in his life."

"Do as my son says," Mrs. Darlington snapped.

Agnes bristled. "Well, I never!" Then came another growl from somewhere in the darkness and she gasped. "Go on, Oliver, what did you want us to do?"

"On my command, raise your arms and shout."

Something emerged from the shadows, its yellow eyes glinting like gold as it neared the firelight, followed by another.

Oliver moved in front of Etta and the rest. "Now!" he bellowed, thrusting his arms into the air.

"Yaaah!" the women roared in unison, their collective voices echoing through the forest. The wolves hesitated, their ears flattening against their heads as they assessed the strange creatures before them.

"Again!" Oliver shouted, and Etta, Agnes and his mother complied, their voices even louder this time. With a final chorus of snarls, the wolves retreated into the darkness, leaving everyone relieved and now on high alert.

Well, everyone except Mrs. Darlington. "What a ruckus. Every outlaw within ten miles probably heard us."

"Would you rather be eaten by wolves?" Agnes shot back. "Land sakes, do you have any idea what could have happened just now? Not to mention that those beasts might come back."

Mrs. Darlington frowned. "I won't have it."

Agnes rolled her eyes. "Oh, for the love of Pete, this isn't England! You can't command a wolf not to attack you."

"She's quite right, Mother," Oliver said. "I'm afraid you'll have to accept that you, along with the rest of us, are in a precarious predicament."

He turned to Etta, and she did her best to stop shivering. Her slender body was visibly shaking from not only the cold, but their recent encounter. She didn't escape outlaws only to get ripped to pieces by wolves. What a sad ending that would be!

"You poor thing. Here, take my jacket," Oliver slipped off his garment and draped it over her shoulders.

Etta looked at him with eyes filled with gratitude and a heavy helping of admiration. "Thank you." She pulled the coat tighter around herself. "I don't know what we'd do without you."

"Think nothing of it," he replied, then scratched his nose. Was he blushing?

Etta smiled and fought the urge to lean into him. She wanted his arms around her, but that wasn't about to happen with Agnes and his mother nearby. No matter— she had more important things to worry about. Like whether Frank and his gang heard their shouting or saw their fire. Maybe the rain slowed them down or forced them to seek shelter somewhere. With any luck, they'd give up their search and leave the area.

Problem was, she didn't think she and the others would get that lucky. As far as Frank and his gang were concerned, Mrs. Darlington, Oliver, and Agnes were all worth a pretty penny, and she had a gut feeling this was far from over.

Shadows stretched across their tiny camp, casting eerie shapes on the surrounding trees.

"Try to get some sleep," Oliver announced, his voice steady despite the fatigue weighing upon him. "I'll keep watch." He just hoped he didn't nod off while doing so. Their brief encounter with a couple of wolves was unnerving enough. What if the beasts came back?

"Oliver..." Etta hedged, her gaze flitting around their dark surroundings. "The wolves... what if they come back?"

She would ask that. "Now don't you worry." He placed a comforting hand on her shoulder, meeting her eyes. "I won't let anything happen to you. We're in this together, and I'm going to get us out of this wilderness safe and sound."

"Thank you," she murmured, a half-smile gracing her lips. Was she relieved to hear it or trying to convince herself it was true?

Oliver pushed the thought aside and clapped his hands, catching the attention of Agnes and his mother. "We should leave at first light. Let's get everything ready for the night. Etta and I will gather more wood for the fire. Mother, Agnes, you stay here and make sure it doesn't go out. It might start raining again."

His mother grumbled, but he ignored it and took Etta's hand. "I'll make a torch so we can see what we're doing. Um, you wouldn't mind parting with some of your petticoat, would you?"

"Oliver!" Mother cried.

"It's for the torch," he sighed, then turned back to Etta. "Well?"

She nodded then bent to her ankles. "I'm not sure I can tear it without a knife."

He bent down and hesitated, hands poised at her ankles. "Erm, could you lift your skirt..."

"Oliver!"

He closed his eyes. "Mother. Stop."

"Oh, good grief," Agnes joined them. She got down on her knees, took the hem of Etta's worn petticoat, then tore into it with her teeth.

Etta gasped. So did Oliver. He'd never seen Agnes act this way before. He also wished he'd thought of it as Agnes pulled at the ruffle of the petticoat with one hand and worked her way around Etta to get as much of the fabric as she could.

When she was done, she climbed to her feet and handed it to him. "Most of it's dry, lucky for you."

Oliver nodded in response, found a suitable dead branch on the ground and tied the torn ruffle around it. He went to a nearby pine tree, scraped off some pitch, and did his best to get it onto the fabric.

"Did the captain teach you that?" Agnes asked.

"Yes." He smiled at her, then motioned for Etta to join him as he lit his makeshift torch and it flamed to life.

"We shan't be long." He took Etta's hand and headed into the trees.

"We're not going far, are we?" she asked with concern.

"Of course not. If those wolves are nearby, I want to be close to the others.

She nodded as she looked for anything that might burn.

As Oliver worked alongside her, he kept a watchful eye on her as they gathered what they could. Each time their eyes met, a warmth spread through him, stoking the embers of affection that had begun to smolder within his heart.

They ventured further into the trees, and Oliver's resolve grew stronger, fueled by the determination to keep Etta safe and rescue her and the others from whatever fate awaited them during tomorrow's trek through the unforgiving wilderness. But first they had to make it through the night.

The forest closed in around them, its tangled under-growth alive with the rustle of unseen creatures, the distant call of night birds and the faint murmur of a nearby stream. Good, they'd find it in the morning and have fresh water.

"Over here," Etta said, crouching by a cluster of plants. "We can eat these."

"Perfect," Oliver said, trying to keep his spirits up. He was more than a little hungry. "What is it?"

"Wood sorrel. Pa called it sour grass. You can't eat

much or it might make you sick, but something is better than nothing."

He examined the clover-like plant. "Very well, pick some, but keep an eye out."

She nodded and got to work, gathering as much as she could. "Oliver," she said, plucking a leaf and scrutinizing it, "You've been a big help. This isn't a simple journey, but we believe in you. Even your mother does."

"Thank you," Oliver murmured, touched by her words. "That means more than you can imagine." Indeed, he was wondering if Mother had any confidence in him at all.

They gathered as much wood as they could carry, along with the plant Etta found, and returned to camp. For the women's sake, he'd forge ahead, no matter the obstacles that lay in wait. He had to get them back to Apple Blossom, then hope and pray they'd seen the last of Frank and his inept gang of outlaws.

He glanced Etta's way and his gaze lingered on her more than once. His growing feelings were driving him to become more attentive to the needs of those around him. Well, there was nothing wrong with that... until Mother took notice. Then he'd have another fight on his hands.

"Oliver," Etta whispered, sidling up to him. "Do you think we'll have enough wood to last us until morning?"

"I'm not entirely sure but if I have to gather more, I will. Tomorrow we'll forage for additional sustenance.

I'm afraid you and Agnes are more familiar with any edible plants and berries than my mother or myself."

Etta nodded. They both knew it was true. He was thankful they ran across the "sour grass." He hadn't tried any yet, but if she said it was edible, she would know.

After a fitful night, the sun rose from behind the mountains, casting long shadows that stretched like grasping fingers across the rugged terrain. Now that they could see where they were, Oliver squinted into the growing light, studying the steep cliff face and the treacherous drop below. It was a good thing none of them wandered too far this way in the dark. They could have stepped off the cliff and fallen to their deaths.

He sighed, hands on hips as he continued to study their surroundings. He knew taking the direct path might be faster, but it would also put them at risk. Etta said there was a river to cross, then they'd have to follow it for a time and cut through a short pass to get back to Apple Blossom.

"Oliver," Etta called worriedly, "are we going to make it to the road?" She was gathering small pieces of wood to start another fire if they needed one.

"Indeed," he replied with a reassuring smile. "I've spotted a trail that should allow us to bypass this perilous slope." He pointed toward a narrow path snaking its way along the cliff side, obscured by overgrown foliage and loose rocks. "It's not without its challenges, but I'm confident we can navigate it safely."

She joined him with a nod of agreement and offered a grateful smile.

Warmth spread through his chest at the sight. "Let's get my mother and Agnes, and proceed cautiously."

They did, and soon Oliver was leading them toward the hidden trail. They went single file, each carefully following the footsteps of the person before them. The path was narrow, but Oliver's keen eye had been accurate —though difficult, it was passable.

As they navigated around the cliff, he had a surge of pride at his own resourcefulness. He knew his brothers would hardly believe his traversing treacherous terrain with confidence and skill, not to mention their mother. If Father could see her now!

Once they'd successfully cleared the cliff side, everyone breathed a sigh of relief, exchanging smiles and words of gratitude. "Oliver, we owe you our thanks," Agnes said warmly. "I've... misjudged you."

"Think nothing of it," he replied with a bashful grin. "It's my duty to keep you all safe, after all."

They continued on, and despite their success, the day's journey had taken its toll on the group. It wasn't long before a sense of foreboding settled in. They hadn't any food other than the handfuls of sour grass last night and would need more water. Their dire situation could only worsen if they didn't replenish themselves.

Oliver had a sinking feeling their journey would only get more difficult from here on out. He glanced over his shoulder at Etta, who trudged along behind him, her face etched with fatigue. Mother and Agnes looked little better.

He concentrated on putting one foot before the other. He had to see them through this ordeal, no matter the cost. In the meantime, he'd hope and pray that his brothers found them before the outlaws did.

Unfortunately, it was already too late.

Chapter Twenty

The scorching sun beat down on Oliver's neck as he stared into the eyes of Frank Lawson, now standing before him. He'd jumped out from behind a rock outcropping and scared the wadding out of Etta and Agnes. How his mother stayed so composed was beyond him.

Frank's appearance alone would strike fear into the heart of any reasonable man. Over six feet tall, barrel-chested and with a face weathered and creased from years under the sun, he looked every bit the villain he was.

Oliver clenched his jaw, his fingers twitching near his hip where he should wear a gun but wasn't. Frank knew it and eyed him with a predatory gleam. Yes, Oliver promised to keep them safe, but here he was staring down the barrel of a gun.

"You've caused me an awful lot of trouble, boy,"

Frank growled, his voice like gravel. He looked at Etta. "You too, Missy."

She swallowed hard. "I aim to cause you a sight more if you don't leave us alone."

Frank barked out a laugh. "Is that so? Or are ya just foolish enough to think yer young fella can take me?" His hand flashed to his gun.

Oliver swore he could hear Etta's heart pounding as sweat trickled down her neck.

A gunshot cracked the air, and Lawson crumpled with a cry, clutching his leg.

Oliver whipped around, as did Etta, and watched his mother lower the smoking derringer in her hand, her face pale but determined.

"Mother?!" Oliver cried.

Frank seized the distraction, drawing a knife and hurling it toward Etta.

Oliver lunged, shoving her aside. Etta screamed as the knife struck his arm. "Oliver!"

He gritted his teeth against the pain, glaring at Frank. The outlaw's eyes widened, realizing his mistake as he looked at Mrs. Darlington. She gave him a humorless smile and fired a second derringer!

For a long moment, Etta could only stare. Frank was clutching his other leg and moaning in pain. She looked at Mother in disbelief. "Where did you get..."

"They've been strapped to my legs," she said, nose in the air. "Trust me, dear, I never go anywhere unprepared." Her eyes skipped over their surroundings. "As

I've only one bullet in each derringer, I had to save them for when we really needed it."

Everyone gaped at her, including Oliver. "Mother?"

She sighed. "For Heaven's sake, Oliver, this *is* the Wild West!"

Etta gaped at her as she touched Oliver's injured arm, her fingers trembling. "Oliver, you're hurt."

He blinked, looking at the weapon that fell from his arm to the ground. "It's not too bad."

"Not too bad?" Etta echoed incredulously. She eyed the knife with dismay. "We need to get you to the doc... oh tarnation..."

"There is no doctor, is there?" Mother spat. "My son could bleed to death out here!"

"Hardly." He gritted his teeth. "You go on ahead. I'll be along directly."

"Don't be ridiculous." Etta looped his good arm over her shoulders, bearing his weight with more strength than her petite frame suggested. "You're in no state to walk alone."

Oliver opened his mouth to argue, but all that came out was, "Ow" as she tried to get him to his feet.

Agnes came to help and between the two of them, they got him up. "What about him?" Agnes asked with a nod toward Frank. He sat whimpering like a deranged puppy, a hand over each wound.

"Oh, dear, he poses a problem," Oliver said. He pulled a handkerchief from his pants pocket. "We'll have to bind his wounds and send someone back for him."

His mother smiled. "I'll do it."

"No!" Frank cried. "Anyone but her!"

Oliver tossed his handkerchief at his mother, who snatched up Frank's gun and handed it to Agnes. "He moves an inch, shoot him."

Agnes nodded, took the gun with her free hand, and pointed it a Frank.

"Do you even know how to use that thing?" he sneered.

"My husband owns a bank, what do you think?"

His face fell. "Oh."

Mrs. Darlington got to work, ignoring Frank's whining.

Etta's brow creased with concern as she examined Oliver's arm again. "You... you saved my life." She cleared her throat and blushed to her toes. "You and your foolish bravery. Land sakes, Oliver, there are easier ways to prove your affection."

He huffed out a pained laugh. "My apologies, darling. I'll try to be less dramatic in the future."

"See that you do." She helped him take a few steps forward. "Now let's get you to town before you bleed to death. I haven't gone through all this trouble to lose you now."

Oliver smiled weakly. "Does this mean you've decided to say yes to my proposal?"

"Proposal," Agnes squeaked. "He proposed?"

"No," Etta said and took in the icy look Mother was giving her. "He... made a suggestion."

"What suggestion?" Mother asked.

He looked at her. "If you must know, I asked Etta if I could court her."

She narrowed her eyes at Etta. "Shouldn't you have asked her father?"

Etta gulped. "My father is dead."

Mother sniffed as she stood. "We'll discuss this when we get back to town." She looked around. "Which way?"

"Do you think someone heard the shots?" Agnes asked no one in particular. She glanced at Frank, who sat, glaring at them.

"We can only hope," Oliver looked at Etta. "Come along, darling. Let's go home."

She clung to him. "You could have been killed."

He grasped her shoulder and gazed into her eyes. "I would brave any danger to stay by your side."

A slow, radiant smile lit her face, and to his surprise, she rose on her tiptoes and pressed a soft kiss to his cheek.

He closed his eyes and held her close in response, not caring what his mother thought. But they still had to make it back to town, and then deal with another threat. His parents. Even if he had found his true love in the tiny town of Apple Blossom, would Mother and Father be the one force on earth that could keep them apart?

In the distance, the thunder of hoofbeats approached. Etta stiffened in Oliver's arms, panic flaring in her eyes. "The other outlaws?"

"I hope so," Frank grumbled. "Then again, maybe I don't."

Everyone glanced his way before turning toward the sound of approaching riders. Etta sighed in relief as a familiar voice rang out: "Oliver! Etta! Are you hurt?"

Sterling and his brothers burst into the small clearing, rifles at the ready. Relief flooded through Etta at the sight of them. "Oh, thank Heaven."

Oliver squeezed her shoulder again. "We're all right," he breathed, then a little louder, "Frank here needs a bit of tending before he goes to jail."

"And the others?" Conrad asked as he dismounted. "Any sign of them?"

"None," Oliver said. "I haven't the foggiest idea where they've gotten to."

Etta caught his gaze, and he saw the determination in her eyes. Together, they would defeat these outlaws. And then, at long last, they would have a talk. He wanted to court her, had saved her! But would he really leave his life in England behind for her? Hmmm, yes, by Jove, he would!

By the time they made it back to Apple Blossom, the sun was setting over the sleepy town. Oliver stood next to his mother in front of the hotel. She had her arms crossed tightly over her chest and a furrowed brow that could rival the Grand Canyon.

"Mother, please, just hear me out," Oliver pleaded,

desperation creeping into his voice as he tried to reason with her.

"Absolutely not, Oliver," she spat, her British accent adding an extra layer of sternness to her words. "You and your brothers have responsibilities back in England. You cannot stay here gallivanting about like cowboys."

"Mother, we have opportunities here that we simply don't have back home," Oliver argued, trying to keep his tone calm. "The rest are in love, true, but we can all make something of ourselves here, build lives for ourselves, including me."

"Build a life for yourself?" his mother scoffed. "And what about Laurel Finchbottom? You know perfectly well that I've arranged for you to marry her. You cannot just abandon your duty to our family and our name."

Oliver's heart sank at the mention of Laurel. She was a lovely girl, but he simply didn't love her. He couldn't imagine spending the rest of his life with someone he didn't have feelings for. But he knew better than to argue about it with his mother. To her, this wasn't about love. It was about duty. "Please, Mother," he said, his eyes searching hers for any sign of softening.

But she remained firm, her arms still crossed. Oliver sighed deeply, knowing that he would have to find another way to convince her.

As they stood in silence, he took a moment to take in his surroundings. The town of Apple Blossom was small but charming. He could hear music and laughter drifting through the air, and the smell of freshly baked pies wafted past him. The town was celebrating the safe return of Etta, Agnes, himself, and even Mother. There would be a gathering in the saloon and the captain was already fiddling with the piano. Not only that, but Flint helped Billy find and recover the bank's money. No mean feat considering six different children had dug up and reburied it.

He drew in a deep breath as the sense of belonging here grew. "Mother, I know this is difficult for you," he said, breaking the silence. "But give us a chance. I promise we won't let you down." His mother opened her mouth to argue, but Oliver cut her off. "Just trust me on this one."

Her jaw went tight. "She's a blacksmith, Oliver. A blacksmith! Think of the scandal."

"What scandal? Conrad's marrying a sheriff, Sterling a rancher, Irving a widow with two children..."

His mother groaned.

"... Phileas an innkeeper and Wallis an undertaker. I dare say, if we don't have the most interesting dinner conversations in the county, I won't know what to think."

His mother remained unmoving and unmoved. "Oliver. You know how I feel about this. I want what's best for you, and that means going back to England and marrying Laurel Finchbottom."

"Laurel Finchbottom?" Oliver scoffed. "Mother, she's nice enough, but her brothers. Besides, Laurel's rather like a dry biscuit. We don't really have anything in common and...

"Oliver!" his mother scolded, her eyes flashing with anger.

"Sorry, Mother," Oliver muttered. "But you have to understand, this is my life. Let me live it my way."

She looked at him for a long moment, her eyes searching his face.

"Mother," Oliver said, using every ounce of charm he possessed. "Just give us a chance here. America is full of opportunities."

"Opportunities?" she huffed. "What opportunities could there possibly be in this wild, uncivilized land?"

"Plenty!" Oliver exclaimed, gesturing around them. "Look at this town. It may be small, but it's full of life. And besides, I've *made* a life for myself here. I have friends, people who care about me."

"Friends won't put food on the table, Oliver," his mother said sharply. "Be it here or in England."

Oliver sighed, frustrated.

Silence settled between them again, the tension palpable. Oliver held his breath, waiting for his mother's response. He didn't want them to part on bad terms, and ideally wanted both his parents' blessing to pursue Etta. But so far he couldn't get his mother to budge.

Just as he was about to give up, a commotion caught his attention. He turned to see Etta and Agnes approaching, a group of townspeople following closely behind.

Etta's face was alight with joy as she caught sight of them, and he felt his heart skip a beat.

"Oliver!" she cried, running toward him. "We did it! Cassie and the others caught the outlaws!"

Oliver grinned, relief flooding through him. "That's fantastic news."

Etta beamed at him, and Oliver was struck once again by how beautiful she was. Her long raven hair was pulled back in a braid, and her cheeks were flushed from the excitement of the day. The sight of her made his heart race.

After being rescued by Sterling and the others, they made it back to town where Captain Stanley tended his arm while the others were seen to by Mrs. Watson and Sarah. Etta excused herself and went to her shop. Mr. Featherstone took Agnes home, and after Mother had a good rest, Oliver found himself with her in front of the hotel, hoping against hope to get her blessing. But it didn't look like that was going to happen any time soon.

"Mother," he said, turning to her. "Aren't you going to say hello to Etta?"

His mother's eyes widened in surprise, and she looked Etta over, her expression unreadable. She hesitated for a moment before taking Etta's hands in hers and examining them. "Rough, calloused. Not the hands of a lady."

Etta's smile faltered slightly, but she didn't pull her hands away. Oliver held his breath, waiting for his mother's next words.

"But strong," Mother added, surprising them both. "A hand that can do hard work and take care of itself. I can respect that."

Oliver sighed in relief, grateful that she was at least willing to give Etta a chance.

"You're the blacksmith," Mother stated.

"I am," Etta said with a nod. "And I take pride in my work."

"I can see that." Mother released Etta's hands. "It's refreshing to see a woman who takes pride in her labors."

Oliver couldn't believe what he was hearing. His mother, who had been so opposed to the idea of him staying in America, was actually warming up to the place. And to Etta.

"Thank you, Mrs. Darlington," Etta said with a smile. "I believe in hard work and doing what needs to be done."

"Good," his mother said with a nod. "You'll need that to make a life for yourself."

Oliver couldn't help but smile. It wasn't exactly a ringing endorsement, but it was a start. A small glimmer of hope that maybe, just maybe, he could convince her to let him stay in America and pursue a life with Etta.

"Well, that's good news about the outlaws," Mother said.

Etta smiled. "Yes, it is, ma'am."

Oliver smiled too, grateful that his mother had at least acknowledged her. He turned to Etta, his heart racing with excitement, and took her hand in his. "I'm so proud of you. Things could have been a lot worse if not for you."

Etta's cheeks flushed, and she looked away for a moment before meeting his gaze. "Thank you, Oliver. But your mother did her fair share."

His eyes flicked to his mother's skirts. "Did Father know you've been armed this whole time?"

She shrugged and looked away. He'd take that as a no.

"Oliver," Etta said softly.

A jolt of excitement shot through him at the sound of his name on her lips. He wanted to lean in and kiss her, to show her how much he cared, but he knew he couldn't do that in mixed company. Instead, he squeezed her hand and smiled at her.

He glanced at his mother and back. Hmmm, maybe he *should* kiss Etta. Right here, right now, and let Mother think what she wanted. He was not marrying Laurel Finchbottom, and that was that. He'd tried being civil; now he was going to have to put his foot down. But first, there was something he needed to take care of.

Chapter Twenty-One

Oliver wiped the sweat off his brow as the furnace flames licked at his face. His arms ached, his back screamed in protest, and his hands were blistered from wielding the heavy hammer all day.

This was not the life he was born to live. His brothers had found their happiness in this small Montana town, but Oliver yearned for the rolling hills of Sussex, for afternoon tea and croquet matches. For a life of leisure as befitted a gentleman. Yet here he was, toiling away in Etta's blacksmith shop like a common laborer. All for the love of a woman.

Etta glanced up from the horseshoe she was shaping and favored him with a smile that made his heart skip. "You're doing a wonderful job, Oliver. My pa would have been proud to take you on as an apprentice."

Oliver grimaced as he lifted the hammer again. "I

daresay your father would not have approved of an English dandy in his smithy."

"Nonsense," Etta said. "You're not a dandy anymore. You're a blacksmith now."

"I'm an embarrassment to blacksmiths everywhere." His injured arm trembled under the weight of the hammer and he struggled to strike the metal at the proper angle. "At this rate, I won't be able to lift a hammer to help with the building of your house."

Etta laid down her tools and came over to grasp his arm. Her hands were as calloused as his, but their touch still sent a thrill through him. "You're too hard on yourself," she chided gently. "Blacksmithing is an art that takes years to master. That you're out here at all, learning a trade so foreign to you, shows me how much you care."

"About?"

She blushed. "Apple Blossom, of course."

"And?"

Her blush deepened as she returned to the anvil where she was working.

Oliver looked into her grey eyes when they flicked to his, and his resolve strengthened. He would bear any blister, any ache, to prove to Etta that he could be the man she needed. The man who would stand by her side for the rest of their days. She just had to believe it.

I won't give up, he promised silently. *Not until I can craft her a wedding ring myself.*

As if hearing him, Etta sent him a smile that lit up the smithy like the brazier flames. He wanted to kiss her, but also wanted this to go right. She was skittish and still didn't believe she was good enough for him. Every time he brought up courting, she balked, then hurried off with some silly excuse. So he'd helped her in the blacksmith's shop as much as he could this week.

This was the fourth day he'd trudged down to the smithy, his muscles protesting with every step. He hadn't realized how physically demanding it would be, and he ached in places he didn't know he had. But the sight of Etta stoking the fire and preparing for the day's work filled him with renewed determination. He would bear any pain to stay by her side.

"Today we have to repair the Smythes' wagon wheel," she said, breaking into his thoughts. "Think you're ready for it?"

Oliver eyed the large wooden wagon wheel propped against the wall. "With your guidance, I can do anything."

Etta's cheeks flushed pink under the smears of soot and ash. "Flatterer. Less talking, more working." But her lips twitched, belying her stern tone.

Oliver set to work, and found that the tasks came easier today. His muscles must be growing accustomed to the exertion, and he fell into a simple rhythm beside Etta. The clang of hammer on anvil, the roar of the brazier, the companionable silence broken by occasional teasing remarks – it all felt so natural. As if he belonged here, by Etta's side. The calluses on his hands had grown, and he regarded them with a mix of chagrin and pride. A reminder of how ill-suited he was for this life, yet also a mark of the dedication that he hoped, would win Etta's heart.

He smiled to himself as he helped Etta lift the newly repaired wheel. Blacksmithing may have been an unexpected path, but it had led him right where he needed to go.

Etta wiped her brow with the back of her hand, leaving a smear of soot behind. "Not bad for your third day. At this rate, you'll be shoeing horses in no time."

Oliver made a face. "Let's not get ahead of ourselves. I'm still struggling with the basics." He ran his hand through his hair, dismayed at how gritty it felt. He'd have to bathe again tonight. The thought almost made him wince. If Mother saw him hauling water up for a bath again, she'd follow him, complaining how he should return to England until he closed the bathroom door in her face. Their recent bout with the outlaws had done nothing to soften her stubborn disposition on the matter.

"Just remember," Etta said. "Blacksmithing is as much art as science. It takes time to develop a feel for working with hot metal. But you've got the dedication, and the strength." She gave him an appraising look. "And you're not too hard on the eyes, either." Her cheeks flamed pink as she tried to skedaddle to the other end of the shop.

Oliver laughed, caught her and pulled Etta close. "Is

that so? And here I thought you only kept me around for my skills at the forge."

"Mmm, maybe," Etta teased. She looked into his eyes and swallowed. "I... should get back to work."

He smiled. She liked his flirting, but he'd just taken it a step further holding her like this. He hadn't kissed her again, not since their time in the woods, but it was getting harder and harder not to. "If there are more benefits like that, I may never want to leave this shop."

"You'd stay here?" Etta said softly. "You'd leave all the pomp and pretense of high society? Your wealth, your estate, everything?" She shook her head and squirmed away. "Your parents are counting on you."

Oliver glanced at the dirty window and the apple orchards that stretched out behind the rustic shop. This tiny Montana town had given him something far more precious than his family's fortune ever could: love, and a place to call home.

"Shall we break for lunch?" Etta asked as she backed away. "I can fetch us something from the saloon."

"No need," Oliver said. "I brought provisions." He retrieved a basket from under the worktable, unveiling cold chicken, bread, cheese and apples.

Etta's eyes lit up. "Well, aren't you full of surprises?"

They went outside behind the shop and sat in the building's shade to eat, a welcome respite from the heat. They ate in silence and when done with the meal, Oliver reclined against a hay bale with a contented sigh. "I can't remember the last time I enjoyed a meal so much."

Etta laughed. "You're getting used to simple pleasures."

A warm feeling blossomed in Oliver's chest. "Speaking of simple pleasures," he said, resting his hands on his knees as he gazed at her, "what are your dreams for the future?"

"Dreams?" Etta's brow furrowed. "I suppose I haven't given it much thought. My only dream was to keep the smithy open after Pa died, and now that's seen to." She shrugged. "Reckon I'll keep on as I have been."

"You could do anything you set your mind to," Oliver said. "If you could do anything, be anything, what would it be?"

Etta looked away, tucking a strand of hair behind one ear. "It's foolish."

"Nothing you say could be foolish." Oliver took her hand, coaxing her to meet his eyes. "Please tell me."

"I... used to dream of having a family of my own," she said softly. "A little house, a garden. Someone to share it with." She squeezed his hand. "But those dreams aren't realistic now."

He pulled Etta into his arms, embracing her fiercely. "They aren't impossible at all," he whispered. "Not anymore."

She pushed him away. "Oliver, no. It's not right, I can't stand in the way of..."

"Of what?" He let her go. "Laurel Finchbottom?"

She cringed. "Such a name."

"Indeed. Trust me, my mother would prefer she become Laurel Darlington."

Etta sighed. "I know."

He tucked his finger under her chin. "We should court."

She scooted away. "After all the flirting you've done with me?"

"Yes. It only proves we should court."

"Your mother would have me shot."

"Never."

She stared at the ground. "I know she'd travel to Virginia City and let the outlaws loose just so she could hire them."

"Come now, darling, you know that's not true." He inched closer, tucked his finger under her chin again and smiled. "Etta, why won't you even consider the idea?"

She stared at him and closed her eyes. "I just can't." She got to her feet and, as usual when he got too close, ran.

Oliver sighed. He may have lost this battle, but he was determined not to lose the war.

The morning sun drenched the windows of the little clapboard church, casting golden light over the worn wooden pews. Etta spied Oliver standing at the front of the chapel, fidgeting with his hat and scanning the space. Was he looking for her?

Her heart leaped at the thought as she slipped into a back pew. She'd worn her Sunday best, a faded blue calico dress that made her gray eyes stand out. They lit up when she saw him, and she smiled as he slowly approached. She wanted to remember him like this—handsome and elegant, every bit the Englishman. "Morning, Mr. Darlington,"

"Miss Whitehead." He bowed. "You look lovely today."

A blush crept over her cheeks. "Why, thank you." They were flirting, and she didn't care. She liked their banter at the blacksmith's shop this last week. But though he thought she was the best thing for him, he was wrong, and it would be only a matter of time before he realized his mistake and wished he'd listened to his mother and gone back to England. She would never be good enough, would never measure up to what his family wanted. If Mrs. Darlington couldn't keep a hold of her other sons, then by golly she'd keep a hold of Oliver. And everyone in town knew it.

As the congregation filled in around them, Etta's courage failed. But how could she let him go? Every time she was with him, she had a sense of belonging she'd never experienced before. Though they were from different worlds, being with him was so right. Still, they'd only known each other a couple of months, and had hardly interacted until recently...

And he deserves so much more than a penniless blacksmith, her mind argued.

She noticed Oliver was staring at her. "What's the matter? You look like you've swallowed a porcupine."

He smiled. "You have such a way with words. It's nothing, darling."

Her heart melted at the endearment as Mr. Watson arrived to give the Sunday Bible lesson. But throughout the lesson, she could only think of one question burning in her mind. What if she said yes to him? What if it was worth risking her heart?

When church let out, Oliver caught Etta's arm. "Might I call on you this afternoon?"

"Of course." She tilted her head. "Is everything all right?"

"Yes, I just... there's something I'd like to ask you. I've some things to do first is all. But I will see you later this afternoon if that's all right?"

She swallowed hard and her knees went weak. "I'll be waiting." She wanted to pull at her hair. She had only a few hours to decide whether she was about to make the biggest mistake of her life. He was going to ask her to court again. Could it be his mother and father were leaving and he told them he was staying behind? Why else would he ask? *Again.* Oh, why was she such a coward?

His mother's disapproving face swam before her eyes, but she pushed the thought aside. This was about her and Oliver and no one else. She sighed. The right thing to do would be to say goodbye, but she wasn't sure she had it in her. Still, she would not run away this time. This time she'd tell him, and that would be that. Otherwise, she would ruin his life and she couldn't live with that.

Etta went home, changed into her work clothes, ate a few apples, then paced the blacksmith's shop. She was so nervous she couldn't help it, but didn't want Oliver to see her like this either, so she went around back and stared at the clearing.

"My house." She could see it in her mind's eye, and suddenly had an image of her and Oliver, along with several children, gathered around the fireplace at one end of the large kitchen. She'd be clearing away the dinner dishes as Oliver played on the floor with their boys. He'd want two at least, and their daughter would tackle him, trying to play as rough as her brothers.

She smiled as it played out in her head. After the kitchen was cleaned and they put the children to bed, they would come downstairs and sit in front of the fire in the parlor and talk about their day. He'd tell her about everything that happened at the blacksmith's shop and she'd tell him about something silly one of the children did. They'd laugh, then kiss, then kiss some more, and soon he'd scoop her into his arms and...

"Hello, Missy."

Etta gasped. Before she could do anything else, a hand clamped over her mouth and an arm snaked around her to pin her to a man's chest. At first she thought it was Frank, but the voice wasn't deep enough. Come to think of it, the body was the wrong size too. Smaller, but no less strong as the man dragged her toward the nearest apple trees, where to her horror his cohorts waited.

Etta was doomed. Herbert, Dale and Dilbert were waiting, the latter holding some rope as Dale pulled a couple of handkerchiefs from his pants pocket. *Oh, no! Not again!*

Yep, again. They had her trussed up and gagged in short order, and tossed into the back of a wagon. They took off through the orchard, cutting their way to the lane that led to the main road. As they were hauling her through the middle of the orchard, no one was likely to hear or see them. As she hadn't been home long, it could be two to three hours before Oliver came to speak to her. That would give Jonny and the others plenty of time to be away with her. She could only hope they'd make the same stupid mistakes as last time.

But considering the evil sneer Herbert was giving her, Etta wasn't sure that would happen.

Chapter Twenty-Two

Oliver was combing his hair when a knock sounded on the door. He sighed. "Yes, Mother?"

His mother opened the door and slipped inside. "Oliver, I hear you wish to speak to Etta." She clasped her hands in front of her. "Don't tell me you're going to tell her you wish to court again?"

Oliver's eyes darted to his mother's face. He knew how she felt about Etta. "Mother, I know you don't like her. But I cannot help it. I love her, and I need to tell her how I feel."

His mother's face softened a bit. "Oliver, I understand that you have feelings for her. But she's not like us. She's from a different world. It won't work out."

Oliver sighed. He knew what his mother meant. Etta was of low social status. But he couldn't help how he felt.

"Mother, I know it won't be easy. But I have to try. I can't just let her go."

His mother shook her head. "You'll be a laughingstock."

Oliver smiled at her. "Thank you ever so much for that tidbit of information." He turned back to the mirror to finish getting ready. "However, that's only if I planned to live in England, which I don't, unless it's my turn."

"Yes, your turn. Sterling told me all about his little rotation plan. What are you, a bunch of crops?" She wrung her hands. "I still think you're making a big..."

She never got to finish as Wallis burst into the room. "Oliver, come quick!"

Oliver spun to his brother. "What is it?"

"It's the Coolidge brothers and their cousin. They must have broken out of jail. Billy said he just saw them take off with Etta!"

His jaw dropped. "What?!" He threw his comb behind him and headed for the door.

"Stop!" Mother cried.

Wallis and Oliver stood in the hall. "Not now, Mother," Oliver said sternly.

She walked to the door and looked her sons in the eyes. "Be sure to take guns with you."

Oliver glanced at Wallis, gave his mother a curt nod and was off like a shot. His heart pounded as he sprinted out of the hotel and headed toward the stables. He couldn't believe what he'd just heard. Etta, taken by the Coolidge brothers? It was unthinkable. Those troublemakers, always causing chaos in their wake, had broken out of jail? And now they'd taken the one person Oliver loved more than anything in the world.

He and Wallis reached the stables and quickly saddled their horses. His four remaining brothers were already there, doing the same. "We'll find her, Oliver," Conrad said, his eyes steely with determination.

Oliver nodded, his jaw set. "We have to. I can't lose her." Finished, he led his horse outside along with the others and mounted. Yes, he was in love with Etta, and when he rescued her, he would not ask her to court this time. He was going to propose. After which he might well beat the tar of those idiot Coolidge brothers! What were they thinking taking Etta? She wasn't worth anything to them, she didn't come from money. The only thing they might be interested in...

He paled and kicked his horse to go faster.

They rode hard, following the wagon tracks through the orchard left by the Coolidges. They weren't hard to spot, nor was the clear path of destruction in their wake. Leaves, small branches and twigs littered the grass between two rows of trees. It was clear they weren't going to stop until they got where they were going. Thank goodness Billy had caught sight of them or they might have had several hours' head start.

Minutes passed as Oliver and his brothers rode, following the trail out of the orchard and onto the lane that led out of town to the main road. When they reached it, the tracks went left instead of right.

"It's no surprise they aren't going toward Virginia City," Sterling said.

Oliver nodded and noticed for the first time that Cassie wasn't with them. He looked at Conrad, who shrugged. "She didn't know," he said. "Though I'm sure by now someone's told her."

"You left the sheriff behind?" Wallis said as they went left.

"I left my betrothed where it's safe. I'll not have my future bride shot at."

The others smiled as they kicked their horses into a gallop and raced down the road after Etta and her abductors.

The ride was long and tense, with each of the brothers lost in their own thoughts. Oliver's mind raced with fear and anger—fear for Etta's safety, anger towards the Coolidge brothers for daring to take her a second time. He couldn't imagine what they wanted with her, but it couldn't be good. They must be upset they got caught and turned over to the law in Virginia City last week. How they escaped was anyone's guess.

The kept riding and suddenly Oliver reined his horse to a stop. "We should have caught up to them by now."

"What if they split up?" Irving asked.

Phileas nodded. "He's right—they could have abandoned the wagon somewhere and set off on horseback."

"But where?" Oliver asked. He studied the road. Yes, there were hoofprints and wagon tracks, but how fresh were they? "Bother."

"We should split up too," Sterling said. "A couple of us can see if they hid the wagon in the brush back there while the rest of us continue this way."

Oliver closed his eyes for a moment. The last thing he wanted was to be on a wild goose chase. But they had little choice if they wanted to find Etta in the shortest time possible. "Fine, we'll split up. Let's go."

The sun sank lower in the sky, casting shadows across the road. Oliver's heart sank as he realized they were losing light, and they still hadn't caught up to the Coolidges. He scanned the horizon, searching for any sign of their wagon.

And then he saw it. In the distance, a small plume of smoke rose into the air, signaling a campfire. Oliver's heart leapt in his chest. They'd found them.

He signaled to his brothers, and they peered at the thin line of smoke snaking its way into the sky. "Do you think it's them?" Wallis asked.

"Considering our last encounter with them," Sterling said, "I'd say there's a good chance. Wallis, head back the other way and see if the Phileas or Conrad found any sign of the wagon yet. Irving, wait here in case any of us need you."

Irving nodded. "I'll be here. How will you signal?"

Oliver sighed. "Just listen for the gunfire."

Etta struggled against her bonds. They didn't make her cook this time. They hardly said two words to her. And that, more than anything, scared her to death. She didn't know what the Coolidges wanted with her, but she knew it couldn't be good. Her mind raced with possible scenarios, but none of them brought her any comfort. She felt a tear escape her eye and quickly wiped it away. She couldn't let them see her cry—she had to stay strong.

Suddenly she heard footsteps approaching. She tensed and wished she wasn't trussed up, but there wasn't much she could do about it. "Hey there, pretty thing," Jonny said, leering at her. "Don't worry, we ain't gonna hurt ya. We just need ya for a little while."

Etta rolled her eyes. "I'm not stupid, Jonny. What do you want from me?"

He chuckled. "Smart and sassy. I like that. You'll find out soon enough." He turned and walked away, leaving Etta alone once again.

She sat, tied to a fallen log, and cursed herself for not being able to escape, for not being able to fight back. But she knew it wasn't her fault. The Coolidge brothers were dangerous and unpredictable even if they were idiots. She had to stay alive, no matter what.

Hours passed and the sun began to set. Good grief, they'd even built a fire. It was as if they wanted to be found. Etta could hear them talking quietly, but she couldn't make out what they were saying. She strained against her bonds, trying to loosen them, but they were tied too tight.

Just then, a gunshot echoed through the surrounding forest, followed by two more. Etta's heart leapt in her chest. Was it the law coming to rescue her? Or had the Coolidges set a trap for Oliver and his brothers? She strained to hear more, but only silence greeted her. She tried to wriggle out of her ropes again, without luck. She felt helpless and alone and realized she was! Where had her captors gone?

Oliver and his brothers, it had to be! They must have fired off a few shots to draw the Coolidges away.

Suddenly she heard footsteps thudding through the grass. Her heart pounded as she braced herself for whoever was coming. At this point it was hard to see. She looked left, then right, trying to gauge where the footsteps were coming from.

A figure emerged from the shadows, and Etta's heart leapt with joy. "Oliver!" she cried out.

"Shh, Etta," he whispered, cutting her free from her bonds.

Etta threw her arms around him, holding him tight. "I thought I'd never see you again," she said, tears streaming down her face.

Oliver held her close. "I'll let nothing happen to you again, Etta. I love you too much to lose you."

She looked up at him, her eyes shining. "You... you love me?"

"I just said so, didn't I?"

"I love you, Etta," Jonny said in a high-pitched voice.

Oliver and Etta froze. She looked over Oliver's

shoulder and saw Jonny, a gun in his hand pointed right at them. "What do you want?"

"What do I want?" Jonny echoed. "I want your betrothed here dead!"

Another shot fired somewhere in the woods.

Jonny made a face. "Looks like I'd better hurry this up. Drop your gun, fancy man."

Oliver did as he asked.

Etta watched Jonny approach and toss a handkerchief at Oliver. "Now gag her. After I kill you, I'm gonna lit out of here with her and have me some fun."

Oliver's eyes narrowed.

"Do it!" Jonny screamed.

Another shot in the distance.

Jonny laughed. "That's right, my brothers are picking your brothers off one by one. This little pigeon was the bait and you fell right into our trap."

"Why are you doing this?" Etta asked. She was so angry a tear escaped, then another.

"On account your man and his brothers ruined our entire career with Frank Lawson!"

Oliver snorted. "What?"

Etta glanced at him, then at Jonny. "What?"

"Just gag her, will you?" Jonny said, waving the gun at them.

Oliver picked up the handkerchief. "I'm sorry, darling."

She nodded in understanding. "Do what you must."

He leaned toward her, his lips brushing hers.

"Ewwww, stop that!" Jonny cried. "Besides, she's mine!"

"Over my dead body." Oliver got to his feet.

"That's the idea, mister." Jonny held the gun high. "Don't come any closer. Gag her!"

Oliver turned to Etta, looked at the handkerchief Jonny tossed him then pulled one from his pocket and tied it around her mouth. He looked at her for a moment, then turned to face Jonny. "I'm sorry, Etta."

She had time to blink once before Oliver lunged for Jonny, tackling him to the ground. The two men struggled for control of the gun. She screamed into the gag, wanting to help, but how?

The men continued to struggle for the gun, rolling one way, then the other. Suddenly there was a shot. She screamed as the two rolled to a stop.

Then all was silent.

She glanced from Oliver to Jonny, her heart pounding.

Oliver groaned and rolled over, then got up and staggered toward her. It only took him a moment to pull off the gag. "Are you all right?"

Etta nodded. "I'm fine. Are you?"

He nodded. "Yes."

"Well, I'm not!" Jonny cried. "You done shot me in the foot, you lowdown snake!"

"You're lucky that's all I shot." Oliver untied Etta and pulled her feet. "Darling."

Before she knew it she was in his arms, being soundly kissed.

"Oh, puh-leeeeze," Jonny whined.

Oliver broke the kiss. "Will you excuse me a moment, darling?

Etta nodded, unable to speak. She could still feel Oliver's lips on hers and wasn't sure she could stand.

Oliver walked over to Jonny as he tried to climb to his feet and punched him square in the jaw. "If you think that was disgusting, wait until you hear this!" He kicked the discarded gun well out of Jonny's reach, walked up to Etta and got down on one knee. "Etta Whitehead, I should have done this last week, but I wanted to spend some time with you, help you in the shop and, well, see if I was any good smithing."

She stared at him then blinked a few times. "Oliver?"

He took her hands in his. "I'm an English nobleman, the youngest of the Viscount Darlington, last in line to inherit. In my world that makes me the least likely one anyone wants to marry. Not with five brothers ahead of me"

Etta glanced at Jonny. He looked like he was out cold. "Oliver... are you...?"

"Proposing? Yes, I am." He squeezed her hands and she was vaguely aware of his brothers riding toward them. "So let me say it again. Etta, I'm not a very good blacksmith but I know you can teach me everything you know. I'll build you a house, just as I promised. We'll live in it, have children and live happily ever after." He looked over his shoulder at Jonny. "Oh, blast it, I was sure that would really get to him, but he seems to be unconscious."

She nodded. "Yes."

He looked at her. "Will you marry me?"

By now his brothers had joined them and were dismounting. Irving went to Jonny and tied him up.

"What about your mother?" she asked.

"I'm sure she'll love coming to visit," he said. "But darling, she's not staying with us."

She laughed as Phileas cringed. "I would be marrying the innkeeper," he muttered.

Etta noticed there were more horses and realized the rest of the Coolidge gang were bound and tied to their saddles.

"Well?" Oliver prompted.

She smiled. "Oliver Darlington. I'd be proud to become your wife. Yes!" She threw her arms around his neck and kissed him.

Oliver smiled. "So does this mean you love me?"

"Yes!" Etta's heart filled with joy and relief. They had survived the Coolidge brothers' dangerous game. Together they would face whatever challenges lay ahead, knowing that they had each other to rely on. A good thing too, considering their biggest challenge was still Oliver's mother.

Mrs. Darlington eyed Etta as she took a seat at the large table in the dining room. The Darlingtons had brought the Coolidge brothers back to town and had them tied up in one corner of the room. They'd lock them up in the captain's storeroom in a few moments, but first they planned to support Oliver and Etta as they faced their greatest foe.

"Marriage, you say?" Mrs. Darlington said. "Don't be preposterous."

Before Etta or Oliver could get in a word, Agnes entered the hotel dining room with Mr. Featherstone in tow. "So it's true! Oh, Etta, I'm so sorry. Are you all right?"

Etta blinked as Agnes hugged her. "Y-yes, I'm fine."

Agnes drew back and looked her over. "Thank goodness." She looked at Oliver. "Thank you." She turned to his brothers. "Thank all of you."

They nodded and blushed as their mother stared them down. "Your father and I," Mrs. Darlington said, "will be leaving Apple Blossom." She looked at Oliver. "And you…"

Agnes held up a hand. "Stop right there." She planted herself in front of the woman. "I have watched your sons endure quite a lot from you, and I won't even begin to tell them what you subjected those poor wretches to." She pointed at the bound Coolidge brothers and their cousin in the corner. "However, your bellyaching managed to drive away their leader that fateful night, and Oliver was able to save us. He protected us from cold, from wolves, and from walking off a cliff, if memory serves. He's quite the man, Mrs. Darlington, and has no small amount of courage. All your sons do." She looked at Oliver's brothers. "I owe you all an apology."

Sterling looked at Oliver, then the rest of his brothers. "You were protecting your own, Mrs. Featherstone."

"No, I was protecting my control." She faced their mother again. "Your sons have saved this town, madam. And we'll all be the better for it. We're not the biggest or fanciest, but we're full of decent people, and if that's not good enough for you, then too bad." She stood straight, squared her shoulders and headed for the lobby. "Come along, Francis."

"Oh, uh, yes, dear." Mr. Featherstone trotted after her.

Mrs. Darlington watched her retreating form as her own husband came into the room. "Was that the banker and his wife?" he asked.

"It was," Mrs. Darlington sighed.

"What did I miss?" Mr. Darlington asked.

She sighed again. "Our sons are getting married. We're staying a little longer."

Oliver's eyes widened. "Mother?"

She met his gaze. "I cannot deny you love, my dears. Agnes is right. You have done this place a good turn and will continue to do so."

"Then you accept our proposal?" Sterling asked.

Etta looked around the room. Letty, Dora, Cassie,

Jean and Sarah had joined them and now stood beside their husbands-to-be.

Mrs. Darlington's shoulders slumped. "So long as you hold up your end, yes. But I don't like it."

"For now," Oliver said as he hugged her. "But you will, Mother, you will."

Etta met Mrs. Darlington's eyes. "Thank you."

"No, thank you, my dear," she said as Oliver released her. She turned to the others. "Thank all of you. In trying to get what I want, I failed to see that you ladies had already given my sons what I sought for them." She squared her shoulders, and headed out of the room. "Come along, Charles."

He trotted after her. "Yes, dear."

As soon as they were gone, Oliver and his brothers burst into laughter, then kissed their betrothed. Oliver looked into Etta's eyes. "Looks like we get to have a wedding too."

"But I don't have a dress."

"Never fear, you will." He bent his head to hers and kissed her.

When he broke the kiss, she looked into his eyes and smiled. "I love you, Oliver. Forgive me for not being braver."

"What? You were abducted twice!"

"But I cowered around your mother."

"Oh, well, yes. She is a formidable foe."

"You ain't gonna lock us up with her, are you?" Jonny whined from the corner.

Oliver smiled. "We're giving her the key and letting her be your jailer."

"No!" Herbert cried. "You can't!"

"I don't wanna be near that woman!" Dilbert groused.

Etta smiled. "Are you really going to let her sit outside the room you plan to lock them up in?"

He leaned toward her ear. "No, but I'm not going to tell them that."

She giggled. "I love you."

Oliver looked into her eyes. "Yes, darling, I know." He kissed her, and the world fell away, leaving just the two of them, the other kissing couples, and four cowering outlaws.

But all Etta knew was that she was in love, and that she and Oliver, along with the other couples, were getting married soon.

THE END

About the Author

Kit Morgan has written for fun all her life. Whether she's writing contemporary or historical romance, her whimsical stories are fun, inspirational, sweet and clean, and depict a strong sense of family and community. Raised by a homicide detective, one would think she'd write suspense, (and yes, she plans to get around to those eventually, cozy mysteries too!) but Kit likes fun and romantic westerns! Kit resides in the beautiful Pacific Northwest in a little log cabin on Clear Creek, after which her fictional town that appears in many of her books is named.

Want to get in on the fun?

Find out about new releases, cover reveals, bonus content, fun times and more? Sign up for Kit's Newsletter at www.authorkitmorgan.com

Printed in Great Britain
by Amazon